Screaming for his mouth to take hers.

"Alexa?" He was using her name as a question. Asking her if he could cross the line. It was there in his eyes.

"Yes," she said faintly.

Lucas moved in slow, as if he was worried she would bolt if he didn't. She wasn't going to go anywhere. Not with the desire to know what his body would feel like on hers. Skin to skin.

Other novels by Fawn Atondo

Chosen series. Chosen Darkness. Chosen Shadows Coming winter 2014

Red series. Office Hours. On Pointe coming winter 2014

FAWN ATONDO

Office Hours

Hush Press

This is a work of fiction. Names, characters, places, and incidents are products of the author's imagination or are used fictitiously and are not to be construed as real. Any resemblance to actual events, locales, organizations, or persons, living or dead, is entirely coincidental.

Published by Hush Press

Copyright – 2014 by Fawn Atondo

ISBN 978-0692263549

www.fawnatondo.com

Printed in U.S.A

For my two beautiful Children, May you always chase your dreams!

And to my Editor Steph, Thank you so much for all your hard work!

To my Readers, Thank you for enjoying my stories! You are the reason I keep writing!

For Brian, You are and shall always be my better half!

Office Hours

OFFICE HOURS

ALEXA

Traffic sucked in LA. There was no other way to put it! Alexa felt the sweat running down her neck and back, and soaking through her tights. At this rate she would look like a drowned Chihuahua by the time she got home! She was half tempted to peel her tights off, right there in the middle of downtown traffic.

Alexa checked the clock on her cell for the tenth time. *Damn*! If she was late for class she would have to stay longer to make up the time her students lost. Making her all that much more behind. Being able to teach was not taken lightly – if she didn't show up on time, she could lose her spot!

Come on! Move people! Slowly, inch by inch, the traffic moved forward, freeing up enough to make it back up to forty-five miles an hour. It wasn't sixty-five, but Alexa wasn't going to complain. Thirty minutes later she was rushing into Points Studio.

Unfortunately for Alexa, she had to work a second job part-time to make ends meet since it wasn't cheap renting a space to teach classes. While New York would be her ideal place to chase her dream, it was not possible to do so there right now. She was in LA because her good friend already had a place for her to stay. So here she was, working her butt off to one day open her own studio.

It was freezing inside the building. Pulling on her long-sleeved wrap, she quickly joined the other dancers on the floor. She'd made it with five minutes to spare! Once they started warm ups at the bar, her mind went onto auto pilot, the movements coming as naturally as breathing.

Class ended at 2:30pm, and since Alexa worked in the heart of downtown she had only one hour to fight traffic and get to work before she was late. Her boss was a weasel-faced guy who didn't take kindly to her showing up even one minute late.

No matter if her reason was legit. He knew she had another job – he'd known it when he hired her. Did this stop him from being an asshole about her classes sometimes making her late for work? Nope. Alexa stopped trying to get the facts across to him.

The office where she worked was part of some new company's start-up. It had more floors than the fanciest hotel she'd ever stayed in, and hundreds of offices. Alexa was not particularly close to any of her co-workers. Her tiny cube, where she spent hours a day typing info into various files, was where she lingered, even at lunch breaks.

Alexa had to admit this was likely the reason she had not made any new friends. LA was full of people but she only claimed to know one of them. Kat was the only person she did anything with, and if not for her, Alexa would have no social life what-so-ever.

Tonight Kat was dragging her along on a forced double date. Kat wouldn't tell her who her date was, simply that she wouldn't be disappointed.

Alexa snorted – that remained to be seen. While Kat did have great taste in the male gender regarding appearance, most of them lacked a personality. Nothing but a nice looking face and some pecs.

Not that she didn't enjoy these, but sometimes she needed to have a conversation more riveting then the beefcakes Kat normally brought around could offer.

Sighing, Alexa pushed aside the thoughts of tonight to finish up her workload of the day. It was Friday and she didn't need anything carrying over to Monday.

The drive home was more relaxing since she had no real deadline. Alexa rolled the windows down letting the warm, slightly smoggy LA air blow in.

As she pulled into their driveway, Alexa thought, as she did every day, what a nice apartment she lived in with Kat. It wasn't cheap by any means but Kat didn't make her pay even close to half of the rental. Kat swore she made more than enough money so Alexa didn't need to worry about paying more than four hundred dollars.

Alexa had to wonder how Kat had got so lucky with her job. The four hundred dollars for everything each month was the reason Alexa had moved out here. Where else could she start the new life she wanted and be able to afford to eat? Kat was a blessing.

Kat was already home, which didn't surprise Alexa as she had great hours, great pay and the freedom to do what she wished. Okay, so maybe sometimes she hated Kat, just a little.

Kat had the music up loud enough to shake the pictures on the wall. The bubbly brunette in question was dancing around the living room in her towel.

"Hey babe!" Kat shouted over the music.

"Hey!" Alexa flopped down on the overstuffed armchair.

"How was work?" Kat danced her way down the hall to kill the music.

"A bitch."

"Your boss still have a stick up his ass?"

"Always and forever," Alexa muttered.

Kat laughed before giving her a hug. Then she flashed her a nice view of her naked bottom.

"That should make your day!" Kat teased.

"Yep, all better," Alexa grinned.

"Get in the shower already, you don't want to look like a sweaty office worker!"

"Kat, I *am* a sweaty office worker!" Alexa pointed out.

"Only part-time sweaty office work. The other half – the half I told your date about – is a sexy ballet dancer!" Kat did a horrible reenactment of a classic ballet pose.

"I teach ballet now, I don't dance!"

"Same thing," Kat informed her with a shrug.

Alexa just rolled her eyes, not wanting to get into what a huge difference it truly was. Her friend wanted her to have fun.

She wanted her to find someone special. Alexa sincerely doubted her date would turn out to be her one true love, but she would do her best to have fun.

Kat had already picked out her outfit for her. A short white skirt with a slight puff, a lacey black shirt and a pair of nude ballet flats.

Alexa laughed. Seemed she was to play the part of the ballerina to the fullest. She did her hair, letting it fall in cute soft blonde curls down her shoulders.

Kat took one look at her and protested.

"Alexa, you're a ballerina. Put your damn hair up in a big messy bun!"

Kat set about doing just that, shoving pins into Alexa's head till she was happy with the results.

"Really Kat, aren't you taking this a little far?" Alexa smiled.

"No, I'm not," Kat retorted, patting her arm.

Alexa was surprised she didn't force her into one of her actual ballet outfits! She was smart enough not to point this out, however.

Nine on the dot they headed down to Kat's Hummer. Yes, the girl drove a freaking Hummer! Alexa drove a very old, well-used Honda.

"Tell me what it is you do again?" Alexa asked jokingly.

"I make people's dream come true!" Kat said with a wink.

"That sounds rather naughty," Alexa observed with a wicked grin.

"It can be sometimes," Kat said.

Alexa was about to ask what she meant by that when Kat's phone started to ring.

"Here, answer this!" Kat said, tossing her cell on to Alexa's lap.

"Um, hello?" Alexa said.

"Hey sexy, where are you?"

Alexa laughed. Clearly Kat's newest man didn't know the sound of his own girl's voice!

"We're on our way."

"We? Sweet, you talked her into it?" The voice sounded amused.

"Yeah, I talked her into." Alexa raised an eyebrow at Kat.

Kat quickly smacked the phone away and grabbed it, managing somehow to barely miss hitting another car as she swerved.

"Okay, we'll see you there," she snapped into the phone before flipping it shut.

"What was that about?" Alexa demanded.

"You're already worked up enough, doll, he doesn't need to add to it," Kat said with grin.

Alexa didn't know what was going on with this blind date. The man was definitely going to turn out to be either really old or super ugly.

Great! Alexa thought with an inward groan.

Pulling up in front of a posh little diner, Kat handed her keys over to the valet and they headed in. Alexa started to scan the tables right away looking for one super-duper hot guy and one old and ugly one.

She saw a couple that could be possibles but the table the hostess led them to was empty.

"They're running a little behind," Kat told her.

"I guess you saw me scanning the masses?"

"Yes, and don't worry, you're going to love your date!"

Alexa just gave her a pointed look. She still was not buying that her date was going to be anything less than a disappointment!

"I swear, this time you will enjoy my pick!"

Sipping her drink a little quicker, Alexa thought if she was halfway to happy town when he arrived she would be able to roll with the punches a lot better.

"God, Alexa, don't turn into a lush!" Kat frowned, taking away the drink the waiter had just set down.

"I am going to need all the help I can get!" Alexa promised Kat.

Kat was about to say something to that, but the hostess coming toward them followed by two men ended her rant.

Alexa took a deep breath then turned to face what fate was lending her tonight. Her eyes shot right pass the first guy to the tall, broad-shouldered one behind him.

"Holy shit," Alexa whispered.

Kat grinned on hearing her words before leaning closer and saying, "I told you so!"

Maybe Kat was right about this one. The guy in question was by far the best looking man she had ever laid eyes on. How did he even get those jeans on? Alexa let out a giggle. Lord, she was already drunk!

"Alexa!" Kat whispered. "Stop acting like a ninny!"

"Right!" Alexa agreed as the man slid in next to her.

Kat was quick to introduce everyone. Alexa shook hands with Kat's date, who was very much what she pictured he would be. Cute, medium built with soft curly blond hair.

The man right next to her had nothing soft and curly. No, he was all hard and dark. He even smelled like a man – the kind of scent you would think those hot cologne guys would smell like!

Alexa had to stop herself from leaning in to sniff him. That surely would seem a little odd. She quickly felt three pairs of eyes on her. Looking up, she wondered what she had missed.

Kat looked amused and so did the rest of their group. Making eye contact with the man next to her, she felt her insides jerk to attention.

"What?" she asked

Alexa wanted to smack herself! What the hell kind of greeting was that?

"Nothing, I just wondered if you figured it out?"

Alexa was not sure what he thought she needed to figure out. Looking to Kat for some help, she found only a huge goofy grin.

"Meaning?" Alex pressed, hoping he would help a girl out.

"If I smell good or not," he answered with a smile.

The smile brought out dimples. Dimples, for crying out loud! What more could possibly make this man any hotter? Oh, she had a few ideas but she shut them down quick.

"You smell wonderful!" Alexa informed him.

He laughed at this before turning to look at his friend. It was a look which meant something but Alexa was not in on the joke. Where they having one over her? The thought was not a pleasant one. Maybe drinking so much beforehand had been a bad idea.

"Sorry, Alexa had a few drinks before you got here to loosen herself up," Kat offered as way of an excuse for her friend's strange behavior.

"No worries, Lucas could use some loosening up too," Kat's man, Mitch, said.

Alexa blushed. She may have had a few but she was well aware what kind of 'loose' he was referring too! Did she want to leave this hanging in the air between them all night? She was loose? Far from it. Nothing was loose on her. She spent hours a day making sure of that through ballet.

"I assure you there is nothing loose on my body!" Alexa informed him tartly.

Kat's mouth dropped a little and her eyes got big before she busted up laughing. Alexa knew she'd just dug herself a bigger smut hole, but whatever, she would not take it back!

"Is that a promise?" Lucas's deep voice asked.

Alexa locked gazes with him. His whisky-gold eyes seemed focused on her mouth. Was he flirting with her? She had promised to have fun tonight. Why not start with some playful banter?

"Oh no, it's a guarantee," Alexa said in the sexiest voice she could.

"I'm tempted to find out, Alexa," Lucas replied.

The look in his eyes made it seem like a warning. Her heart sped up, slamming into her ribs. Alexa was not going to back down. If this was a challenge he was throwing down, well, she would play.

"Words are cheap," Alexa told him, with a bat of her lashes.

His lips parted into a smile before he mastered his skill of being blasé once more. He draped an arm around her shoulders before leaning in, bringing his lips next to her ear. So close his warm breath fanned her neck.

"But I'm not, I'll pay full price," he whispered into her ear, his lips touching her skin for one light-as–a-feather caress before he leaned away.

Alexa didn't have a comeback to that but she was saved from the worry of it by Kat bringing up the club they would be going to. Lucas moved back to his side fully, but still Alexa's skin burned where his lips had touched. Another round of drinks and they headed to the club.

It was only a block down from the diner so they walked. Kat wrapped around Mitch like a human shawl. They kept stopping to make out every few feet, forcing her and Lucas to stand waiting like peeping Toms for them to stop. Once they made it to the club the cool air had returned some of Alexa's reserve.

Lucas didn't seem like he wanted to dance. He kicked back at their table with his drink, content to chill right there.

Alexa too stayed at the table, sipping at her gin, but still debating whether she should drink any more.

Would it be worth it come morning if she let go fully? She had not crossed many moral lines in her life, but if there was ever a time, it was now.

Alexa looked over at her date and found him staring at her, those eyes roaming over her like she was dessert. Did she want to be his something sweet tonight?

Lord help her – if she melted at a mere touch of those full lips, what would happen if he really kissed her?

Lucas got to his feet holding out his hand to her. *Oh crap*! Alexa thought wildly as he dragged her out onto the dance floor.

The beat pulsing through the room and heat from the other couples moving around them made it suddenly very, very hot.

"It's kind of hot in here," Alexa choked out.

"Getting cold feet?" Lucas asked.

"No, I'm just saying…" she began, but Lucas cut her off.

"Talk's cheap… Remember?"

With those words, Lucas pulled her close to his body. So close she felt every hard firm part of him. The song was slow but seductive.

Alexa was a dancer – her body reacted of its own will. Lucas's eyes lit with fire as she moved her body against his.

He brought his hands to her hips, gripping her tightly as she twisted them. Her head pressed to his chest and she could hear the strong beat of his heart. It was the most sensual dance of her life and she did it with a total stranger. Others stopped to watch them work around one another.

"You're right, there is nothing loose on your body," Lucas told her roughly.

"Yours either."

Lucas brought his lips down to capture her mouth in a kiss. The kiss sent electric shocks rolling down her stomach to her toes.

Lucas pulled her even closer and she felt his hard cock pressing into her thigh. His mouth kissed down her cheek to her neck.

Normally she would be ashamed to be doing this in front of a club full of people, but she couldn't think with him kissing her like this.

"My place?" he whispered.

Alexa could only nod as they made their way toward the table to grab their belongings. Kat was there, waiting for Mitch.

"You leaving?" she asked.

"Oh yes," Alexa said.

"Alexa... have fun," Kat smiled.

"You too, see you later."

Alexa accompanied Lucas out of the club and back to his car. She wasn't sure what make it was but it looked expensive. She had a brief moment of doubt about going off with him.

"Promise me you're not a crazy person," Alexa said.

"I promise," Lucas assured her, with a laugh.

"Good, me either, so you know."

"I wasn't worried," he assured her.

They got into the car and he pulled out onto the road leading toward Santa Monica.

Alexa was a little shocked when he pulled up to a beach front resort. Who lived at a resort? Lucas got out of the car, coming round to open the door for her just like a proper gentlemen should.

"You live here?" Alexa paused, her hand still on the door of his car.

"For the time being."

Lucas led her into the lobby and straight to the elevator.

Alexa felt ten shades of red as she fought her moral code. Who went with a stranger back to his place to have sex? Who did that kind of thing? Okay, Kat did, and she was still a good person, Alexa reasoned with herself.

Still, Alexa wasn't Kat! She was the good girl, the girl who put her dreams first over sex and boys. Not the girl who got tempted by a handsome face. *We are not having sex*! Her inner voice warned her as the elevator door binged open.

Alexa was in full agreement with her inner voice. She wasn't going to give it up to Lucas, no matter how hot he was. *Maybe a few kisses. A few kisses wouldn't do any harm!*

"You need to see this view."

Lucas's words pulled her from her inner battle and she came to look out the large bay window. It showed off the Santa Monica coastline in all its glory.

"It's beautiful," Alex said, turning to look up at him.

He was so close. Too close for her reasonable side to stay focused, especially not when her inner temptress was screaming for his mouth to take hers. For his hands to touch her. Lucas's golden stare ran over her body in such a way her skin tingled.

"Alexa?" He was using her name as a question. Asking her if he could cross the line. It was there in his eyes.

"Yes," she said faintly.

Lucas moved in slow, as if he was worried she would bolt if he didn't. She wasn't going to go anywhere.

Not with the desire to know what his body would feel like on hers. Skin to skin.

He moved his fingers to her bun, pulling free the pins and letting her curls fall around her shoulders. Once her hair was free, he moved to the buttons on her shirt. One, two… Alexa counted them as he undid them.

He moved his hands under the material, careful not to touch any skin, as he pushed her shirt off and down her arms. Next his hands slipped over her skirt, feeling for the zipper at the back. With one tug it slid down. The skirt fell to the floor.

She was now standing there in front of him in nothing but her bra and panties. He didn't say a word. His eyes kept hers locked in a gaze. He removed his own shirt, showing just how well toned he was. Hard muscles danced in the soft city lights.

He undid the buttons of his pants. All too soon he was standing in front of her bathed in a mix of shadow and light but nothing else.

No boxers, no briefs. Alexa swallowed, her gaze breaking from his to take in all of him. He was perfect. Alexa forced herself to look up at his face once more.

Lucas closed the distance between them quickly, walking her back into the glass window. The coolness of the glass pressed into her back. He took her lips in a slow kiss. It grew more demanding as his hands worked the clips on the back of her bra.

He pulled it down her arms, letting it drop to the floor with the rest of her clothes. His hands cupped her breasts, testing their fullness in his hands. His lips grazed down her neck to her collarbone.

"I want you." His words were thick with need.

Alexa couldn't speak. All she could do was wrap her fingers in his thick hair, bringing his mouth back to hers. The stern talk she gave herself about no sex went straight out the window.

Lucas deepened the kiss as he worked her fingers free from his hair to trap them above her with one hand. With the other, he pushed aside the lace of her panties to put one finger inside her.

Alexa gasped into his mouth but Lucas didn't stop the kiss or the movement of his finger. The need building inside her grew more intense. Lucas let her hands go and Alexa wound them around his neck.

She had never touched a man before. One time in high school she had gone all the way but her clothes had stayed on and so had his. It was over fast and it was nothing to write home about. But this. This was different!

Alexa was shy, but her desire to touch Lucas was stronger. She needed to touch his hard flat stomach.

So she did, enjoying the intake of his breath. Her knuckles skimped over his hardness. Alexa froze. Then slowly, oh so slowly, she wrapped her hands around Lucas's cock. His body jerked in response.

His lips moved from hers to nip a trail down her shoulder and lower to taste her breast. Her head rolled back on to the glass. Lucas stopped his touch on the most intimate part of her to grip her bottom.

"Wrap your legs around my waist," Lucas said roughly.

Alexa did as he told her, her legs locking over his hips. Lucas pushed her more firmly into the window as he moved aside the lace at her opening one more time. Instead of a finger, he pushed his hard cock into her softness.

Alexa stopped breathing for a second as Lucas's hardness thrust into her body. A strange sensation grew as he moved all the way inside her, but the feeling of pleasure replaced it as Lucas rocked his hips. She moaned.

"Lucas." She was breathing heavy.

He brought his mouth back to hers, biting softly on her lower lip. One hand on her back, the other pressed next to her head on the glass.

"Move with me, Alexa."

She did. He started to move faster, thrusting into her harder each time, stealing her thoughts right from her head.

Alexa was making all kinds of sounds. Sounds she didn't even know she could. Purring was not a normal sound for her, surely!

"Come on, baby, stay with me," Lucas murmured in her ear.

Stay with him? Oh God, she couldn't promise that! Not with her mind and body splitting apart with every thrust!

Alexa could feel a fire burning deep inside, growing every time Lucas moved. She was shocked for a moment when Lucas pulled free, letting her slide down the window back to her feet.

 She wasn't able to worry about it though. Lucas turned her around so this time she was facing the glass.

He slid back into her, this time from behind, taking a firm grip on her hips. He moved hard and fast now, building up that fire from before to something even hotter. Alexa was trying to hold back the scream which ripped through her body as the orgasm hit her.

Alexa shouted Lucas's name so loud she felt the vibration from her cry through the glass pressed to her cheek.

Her own name echoed for a moment after Lucas found his fulfillment. They stayed like this, her pressed into the window and him leaning into her.

When Lucas did move back, he only pulled her to the cream-colored sofa to start a slower assault on her senses. He touched and kissed her till once more raw passion was burning between them.

At some point during the night, Lucas got up to take a shower. Alexa passed out.

Waking to the bright sunlight of day, she stretched, got up and dressed in her crumpled clothes from last night. Lucas was nowhere to be found. Finally she saw a note on the dining table.

ALEXA,

Thanks for last night.

Alexa stared at the one-line note. She wasn't sure how to take it, seeing how she had never done a one-night stand before. Under the note was an envelope also addressed to her. She was feeling uncomfortable being at his place alone so she slid it into her purse and left.

Once outside she called Kat.

"Hey doll! How was last night?" Kat asked

"Great, I had fun. Umm, could you come pick me up?"

"Sure thing. Where are you?"

"Sunset Resort in Santa Monica."

Kat didn't ask anything else and Alexa was glad Kat wasn't the kind to pry.

When Kat did show up, all she did was talk about how much fun she had with Mitch. Alexa offered up that she too had a good time with Lucas. They left it at that.

Back home Alexa showered. By the time she was finished and dressed, she was feeling like herself again – just as long as she could keep the events from last night from replaying in her head.

Alexa sat on her bed, finally getting to the envelope Lucas had left for her. She slid her finger across, ripping it open.

 Alexa was stunned at what greeted her eyes. Bills! Lots and lots of fresh, crisp, green bills! She froze, eyeing the money, while a sick feeling grew in the pit of her stomach.

"What the hell?" Alexa whispered.

Alexa ran her fingers through the thick wad of cash. This was a lot of money, but why would Lucas pay her? Did he think she was whore?

The idea didn't sit well and a snicker from her inner voice played like fingernails on a chalk board.

See, only whores move that fast!

It was not a reassuring thought and she smashed it out like an old cigarette butt. She was not going to keep this money! No way! If anyone knew how to reach Lucas, it would be Kat.

"Kat!" Alexa called out.

The sound of feet padded down the hallway as Kat made her way to her room. Flinging the door open with her normal zest, Kat came in and plopped down on the bed.

"What?"

Alexa didn't say anything. She just picked up the envelope and dumped the bills out all over her bed. Kat jumped up so fast she nearly rammed her head into the lamp behind her.

"Holy shit, Alexa! Where did you get that?"

"Lucas."

Kat's lips made a perfect O as she stared from the bills on the bed back to Alexa.

"Lord," Kat breathed, looking once more at the money.

"Yeah, lord! Why would a man leave his date this much money? Even for a one-night stand? Is this some kind of a joke, or an insult?"

Alexa had to wonder what had made Lucas do such a thing. Clearly a normal person wouldn't carry around this much money, so he'd known before they even went out that he was going to pay her. And then things started to click in her head.

Alexa saw that Kat was watching her with a pinched look, as if she was worried about answering her questions. Why would she be so on edge about Lucas leaving her money? Unless...

"Kat, what is it you do? I mean for real, no cute comebacks. What is your line of work? Exactly?"

"I'm a PIMP girl."

"You're a what?" Alexa gasped, not believing she had heard right.

"It's a company that hires out beautiful woman as dates for really rich guys, and sometimes gals," Kat said.

"You're a call girl?" Alexa asked in shock.

"No, nothing like that, we merely pose as dates, but some girls, some of the time, take a little more too... you know," Kat said with a wiggle of her eyebrows.

"Do you take the little extra, Kat?"

"Once in a while, if I like the date."

"Is it possible Lucas thought I was a... PIMP girl?" Alexa didn't want to say whore, even though it was what she was thinking!

"I might have led Mitch to think you worked with me..."

"You fixed me up with a guy who thought I would have sex with him if he paid me? Dammit, Kat! Why would you do that?"

"I'm sorry, I didn't think he would go that far. Mitch said Lucas was super picky and I didn't think he would go all the way! And I definitely didn't think you would! I just wanted you to have a good time."

Alexa was not sure what to say. On one hand, she was super pissed at Kat for getting her into something like this. On the other, if Kat had thought it would be a fun date for her and nothing more, could she blame her?

Hell, yes she could, Alexa told herself. If Kat had warned her about what was going on, she would not have let it go that far. Now she'd slept with a stranger and got paid because he thought she was a damn call girl!

"I'm really pissed at you, Kat. I'm not letting you off the hook for this!"

Kat's eyes sparkled with unshed tears as she took Alexa's hands into hers.

"I'm truly sorry, I should have told you. You're right."

Alexa took a deep breath. Letting it out slowly, she looked at her best friend who sat there looking like a wounded puppy.

"I accept you're sorry, Kat, but I'm still mad. But I love you," Alexa said, squeezing her hand.

Kat wiped away a lone tear before she broke out her best sunny smile.

"Thank you! I promise not to do anything remotely close to this again."

Alexa rolled her eyes before playfully swatting at Kat.

"Yeah, be sure you don't! Now, how do I reach Lucas to give him back his money?"

Kat sighed before pulling her cell phone free from her back pocket. Scrolling through her contacts, she turned it to show Alexa Mitch's number.

"But before you do this, why not keep the money?"

"No, Kat!"

"Hear me out. The man doesn't know you, you don't know him. So what if he thinks he paid an escort girl for sex? You know you're not a PIMP girl. Look, that money would do wonders for you. You could use it to open your own studio, couldn't you?"

Alexa knew exactly how expensive it would be to open a studio. Her classes to become a professional ballet teacher were not cheap either, especially not when she wanted to launch a highly accredited school.

One that got girls great leads and jobs without them having to look like a walking set of bones. It had been her dream, her goal, since she had dealt with these body image issues firsthand as a dancer.

Yet she wouldn't – no, couldn't – keep this money and still feel like a decent human. Could she? Alexa ran her hand down her face. It was too much to try and think about.

"Want me to call?" Kat asked.

"No, put it away. I'm going to have to think about this."

Kat grinned, laying back on the bed now. She fanned herself with some of the money, doing her best to tempt Alexa to keep it.

"I haven't said I was going to keep it!" frowned Alexa.

"But you haven't said no yet, either!" Kat reminded her.

Alexa felt her inner voice trying fight its way out. To tell her how bad a person she would be if she did keep this 'sex' money.

She wasn't going to deal with her own snide self. Not right now. Instead she wanted to find out what info Kat had on Lucas. Shouldn't she at least make sure he wasn't a flipping serial killer first?

"Why would Lucas need to hire a date? He seems perfectly capable of finding his own," she said.

Alexa didn't miss the look that crossed over Kat's face.

"OMG, there's something wrong with him! Isn't there?"

"No, nothing horrible, he has... issues."

"Issues? What kind of issues?" Alexa's heart was thumping hard.

"He isn't a crazy person or anything. He's, um, he's a sex addict."

Alexa was lost for words. Speechless. Lucas was a sex addict? What did that even mean?

"You hooked me up with a sex fein! Perfect!"

"No. Yes, well, maybe. But he is a picky sex fein. Mitch said he rarely hooked up with a woman he'd only just met. But he needs to get laid and doesn't do the whole girlfriend thing because of his issues."

Alexa processed this for a moment. Of course, she would be the one to be attracted to a man with a sex addiction! Yet, was it really a bad thing? Alexa was starting to see things in more than black and white and she didn't like it!

LUCAS

Lucas wasn't a patient man. He wanted what he wanted now. This waiting around for the perfect moment was not in his DNA. Yet Mitch had pointed out that, for the good of his company, he needed to play this out slowly. Wisely. It was damn annoying is what it was!

Every day he worked his ass off behind the scenes, building up his business, and thanks to one bad choice on his part, and a lifetime of them on his father's, he couldn't link his name to his own company! Lucas tapped his pen a little harder on his desk till it ended up snapping. Blue ink dripping down on to his slacks.

"Hell," Lucas swore before tossing the bent pen in the trash.

He had two choices on what to obsess about: work, or one hot, tight, leggy ballerina! With eyes clearer then a spotless Los Angeles sky, he was hard pressed to forget her. He was tempted to have Mitch call up the PIMP agency and set up another go around for him.

Alexa had not been what he had expected her to be. The way she moved told him right away she had definitely been a ballerina at some point. If she still was, he couldn't guess, but the facts Mitch had shared about her not partaking in the act of sex with her clients made him willing to go see what this so-called dancer had to offer.

She was more than he had hoped for. Her dark blonde hair had been pinned up in a messy bun, and a few crazy curls had come loose to tease the nape of neck.

Lucas had wanted to take her home right then, but he'd got the vibe she wasn't ready yet. Once she'd showed the first sign of wanting him, he'd taken the lead.

Her body was hard everywhere. No slack, no fat. Yet she was not lacking curves. Her hips were rounded and her breasts full. Nothing like one would picture a ballet dancer. His dick grew hard just recalling the way she felt.

He was not one for dating: he refused to get close to a woman. One had nearly brought down everything he had worked for. And his father had lost it all due to his lack of control when it came to the fairer sex.

Lucas was not going to be one of those men. The kind who let a pretty face and a pair of nice tits knock him on his ass. He knew firsthand how gossip could ruin a man's life. He'd faced it because of a pretty face. His mother might have taken everything his father had and run it into the ground, but his father had let her. He was weak. Lucas was not. No, his mistake was underestimating the crazy depths some women could sink to.

Lucas pinched his nose between his fingers and forced the past back into the dark hole it had climbed out of.

He was not going to play that drama over again. He had learned his lesson. Women could not be trusted. A few might be decent enough, he supposed, but he hadn't run into one. All he wanted from the opposite sex, was, well, sex. A man needed to get laid from time to time.

Mostly he hooked up with random girls he met at clubs and bars. Mitch's new-found pastime seemed a little much.

Why pay a beautiful woman for sex? Mitch was no loser and he didn't lack in the looks department either, yet he swore about using the girls from PIMP. While the agency didn't explicitly hire out their girls for such a thing as sex, many of them would cross that moral line if the payment was right.

The PIMP agency didn't get involved and the women pocketed all the earnings from such transactions. Lucas didn't think the name helped set these woman apart from whores, but if the company wanted a humdinger of a name, well, they'd done a great job! Lucas now had to agree that if the women all looked like Alexa then maybe paying for their company was not so far out there.

Of course, he couldn't let such acts get around to the press or the other board members. He was working his squeaky clean reputation back from its falsely tarnished one, and didn't need paying for sex to be added to his résumé.

Thankfully Alexa didn't know anything about him other than his name. And only his first name. As long as he kept it this way, he could enjoy their time together without worrying about word getting around.

Since he wasn't getting any work done anyway, he dialed up Mitch.

"Hey man." Mitch sounded out of breath.

"Is this a bad time?" Lucas had to wonder if he was interrupting anything.

"No, just doing a work out."

"Ah, well, er, do you know how to reach Alexa?"

Mitch chuckled.

"Yeah, I can call up Kat."

"Great, set up a time for me."

Lucas didn't wait to hear if he would or not. He ended the call and headed back to his place to shower. He kept two addresses: one was personal – he didn't bring girls back there – and the other was at Sunset Resort. He didn't want any lines getting blurred.

He had just gotten dressed when his cell stared to ring. He knew it was Mitch. He slid the screen over.

"What time?"

"Dude, Alexa isn't up for anything tonight. Sorry man."

Lucas closed his eyes. He wasn't going to let her avoid him.

"Call her back and tell her I will double the payment."

"Shit man, you got it bad," Mitch said with a whistle.

"Just call her back."

Lucas stood at the bay window watching the sun set beyond the water. He couldn't fathom her turning him down. He had no doubts Alexa would be tempted by the money now. What woman wouldn't?

His screen lit up once more with Mitch's name.

"The time?" Lucas asked

"Kat told me to have you call."

Lucas swore softly under his breath. He didn't want to call, didn't want to make it personal. Yet he didn't want to call the agency and end up paying even more when all he wanted to do was fuck Alexa anyway.

"Fine, give me her number."

Mitch did and Lucas punched it into his contacts and hit save. It was a seminal moment. He'd never had a woman's name saved in his contacts. Till now.

Alexa answered on the fourth ring. Her voice was husky and he couldn't help but picture her naked on her bed. Had she been touching herself thinking about him? Was this the reason her voice sounded so silky?

"Alexa, I assume you heard my offer?"

He could hear her breathing. It was fast.

"I did. But I am not free tonight Lucas…"

He cut her off.

"Alexa, I will pay you three times as much if you let me have you for tonight."

"Wow." Her soft voice gasped into the phone.

"You know you'll have a good time. I promise to be more attentive than last night." Maybe the pace hadn't been to her liking? This time he would make sure to drive her mad with his hands and mouth.

"Lucas, you can't mean it."

"Can't mean what? The price? Or the fact I can and will fuck you senseless?"

Another soft gasp and he could almost hear her inner will breaking down. She was tempted. Lucas smiled, knowing what she would say next.

"Okay." Her voice once more dipped into something sensual.

"Perfect. I will met you at my place in two hours. And Alexa?"

"Yes?"

"Dress in something that is sure to knock a man dead."

Lucas hung up. He pictured her standing there holding the phone and thinking about what she would wear just for him.

The time dragged by. It was nearly an hour since he had gotten off the phone with her. His eyes kept coming back to the clock.

It was approaching two hours and he was about to call her again when he heard the knock.

Lucas opened the door. Alexa stood there, wearing pink ballet shoes and a long black jacket. He had to wonder what was under it. Nothing? Something naughty?

"I'm not sure what knocks you dead, Lucas, but I came prepared to put on a show."

Her eyes danced with something seductive.

"Can you put this on?"

Alexa handed him a CD.

Lucas walked over to his laptop, the only thing he had here to play music. He slotted it in the drive and waited. Alexa moved to the open area in front of the sofa. Lucas took a seat to watch her.

The first notes of music filled the air and Alexa posed on her toes, her back curving to one side, her arms gracefully twisting above her. Then she kicked one leg out, leaping to land on her toes once more.

Alexa moved around the floor in a graceful manner, fit for a performance on the best stage. She did moves he had no hope of naming, yet he knew they were, without doubt, perfect.

Then the music took on a new tone and Alexa started to move differently. She gyrated her body like she had at the club. She removed her jacket.

She was wearing nothing but a white silky leotard. It hugged her body so tight he could see her nipples through the thin material across her chest. Lucas swallowed. He couldn't take it any longer. He needed to touch her.

Lucas had to remind himself he was going to make sure he drove her insane. Stopping in front of her, he knelt down. Alexa tried to take a step back but Lucas grasped her hips, holding her in place.

"Lucas?" Her tone was slightly apprehensive.

"Alexa, tonight I play the role of pleasure fulfillment." He reinforced his words by placing a light kiss on her inner thigh.

Lucas continued to kiss up her thigh. Once he ran into her clothing, he stood up and pushed the leotard down till he slid it off her legs. Such long shapely legs. He ran his hands over them, enjoying the feel of her firm hard muscles.

Her chest rose and fell as he moved his hands higher. Gripping her butt he kissed a path down her neck across the top of the flesh peeking over her bra. It looked as though her breasts were dying to spill free, so he helped them.

She had no panties on and he was a little surprised she bothered with a bra, but it was only an afterthought as he made a feast out of her nipples.

The low husky sounds she made had his cock pressing hard against his jeans.

"Lucas! Please, I can't take it!" Her plea came out in short breathless words.

"I'm not finished with you yet." His tone was as wicked as it was dark.

He was a man consumed. He wanted to taste every inch of flesh on her body. It was not his normal reaction to sex with a woman.

He took what he wanted, giving just enough to them to reach a climax. He didn't go for above and beyond.

With Alexa he wanted to make her break apart in his embrace, to feel her responses to him with every touch, lick, and stroke from his lips, his hands and, lastly, his cock. He would give her more pleasure than one woman could handle.

He once more took up a spot in front of her on his knees. His lips kissed a fiery trail across her flat stomach to the very core of her. He used his fingers to spread her apart so his tongue could taste her. Light, fast and soft licks at first.

When her fingers sank into his thick hair, he pressed his lips deeper, kissing her in the most intimate way a man could kiss a woman. He kept up his rhythm, forcing her body to its first climax of the night with nothing but his mouth.

Lucas gently eased her to the soft rug. Her long golden hair tangled around her face, her lips so red and so kissable.

His fingers came to replace his mouth, and he moved them, pumping in and out of her. She arched her back, making his fingers sink deeper into her warmth.

He took her lips in a slow kiss. To see her tasting her own juices on his lips made for a hot pulse of pleasure jolting him in his gut.

He wanted to sink into her soft opening so bad, but he would not do so till she was gone. Lost in her own passion.

"Damn Alexa!" he growled, as he kissed her harder.

Her hands gripped his chest, her nails digging into his skin, making him wish they would sneak lower. Yet he would make no move to make her touch him. This was about her. Tomorrow was soon enough to make her do the things he wanted her to do to him.

"Lucas! God please, now!" Alexa demanded.

"Now?" he teased her by moving his fingers.

"Yes, God, yes!" she screamed at him.

"You want me to fuck you, Alexa?" Lucas asked, grazing his lips down her throat.

"Yes!" she agreed eagerly.

Lucas looked at her and she did look more than ready for him. Her whole body quivered as her hips moved with his fingers. He slid one finger out and then quickly put it back watching her mouth gasp in a perfect O.

"Come here then," Lucas ordered.

He stood to remove his jeans before he sat on the floor with his back to the sofa.

Alexa got up onto her knees. Lucas pulled her onto his lap, putting one of her legs on either side of his waist. He gripped her hips, lifting her, before he dropped her on to his hardness. She was so wet he slid in with ease.

She was so tight, so perfect. He nuzzled his face in her neck as he moved her up and down on him. Her arms wrapped around his neck.

He kissed her shoulder before biting her softly. He quickened the pace. Her head rolled back, her hair brushing his thighs.

He kept his hips moving at the pace he had set but slid his hands up to her hair. He pulled softly, getting another soft moan from her. He forced her face back up to his. Locking eyes with her and seeing the fire burning so bright in those impossibly blue eyes, Lucas's stone self-control slipped.

He was no longer judging her passion or his – he was lost in the moment, feeling her, seeing her. Lucas acted on raw lust. He was moving too fast, and he didn't pick up on her orgasm as it hit her. He was lost in the woman, not the act.

He came so hard and fast he felt his chest tighten in an odd way as he spilled his seed. The aftermath of emotion was a shock to him as it rolled through him. He held her to his chest, placing soft kisses to her head.

This was not something he did after sex. He didn't cuddle, or linger in the moment. Yet here he was, enjoying the feel of Alexa on him. Lucas slowly pulled out. Heading to the bathroom to remove the condom, he left her stretched out on the floor.

He looked in the mirror: the flush to his face and the light in his eyes were those of a man happily fucked. Not fucked for the need of it but for the pleasure of it. It was the look of being needed, wanted and desired.

"Fuck," Lucas muttered to his refection.

He splashed water on his face, trying to wash away the feelings Alexa had brought on. He should show her the door and forget her face. But it was not going to happen, not right now anyway. He wanted more of her. Later, when he was through, he would cut ties. They would not have anything more than causal sex.

A small nagging in his gut called his bluff. Lucas refused to acknowledge it, however. *It was nothing but great sex*! he told himself. *Nothing more*.

Alexa was still on the floor where he'd left her. Her eyes opened when he walked in. Those eyes sparkled a clear tropical blue.

"So now what?" Alexa asked him.

Now what indeed? Lucas wasn't ready for round two, not yet. However, he didn't want to send her home either.

"Why don't we have a drink?" Lucas suggested, going to get a bottle of champagne from the fridge.

When he came back, she had her clothes on again. He smiled. For a girl who hired herself out, she was very modest!

"Thanks," she told him, taking the glass.

"You're welcome. Did you enjoy this time… better?"

A blush spread across her face and she stared at the bubbles in her glass.

"Yeah. I mean it was better than before… I get it now," Alexa smiled shyly.

Lucas didn't have any idea what she was talking about.

"Get what now?"

Another blush, this one darker.

"Why you could have a condition like yours. Sex can be really good."

Lucas raised an eyebrow. A compliment, he guessed, but what condition was she talking about?

"Condition?" he pressed.

"I know about your sex addiction," she replied, confused.

Lucas felt his face tighten. *What the hell was she talking about?*

"Who told you I had a sex addiction?" Lucas's voice was flat.

"Mitch told Kat who in turn told me. I'm okay with it, don't feel embarrassed." Alexa reached over and patted his hand.

He wasn't sure if he should laugh or be pissed. Did Mitch really tell his hired lay he was a sex addict? He didn't know what to say to this.

"I don't have any such thing, Alexa."

"Lucas, you don't have to lie to me. I don't care."

"Christ, Alexa, I truly don't have any issue like that. I need sex as much as a normal healthy man – nothing more, nothing less."

Alexa looked puzzled.

"If this is true, why would Mitch tell Kat you didn't date because of your issues – that you were super picky but you needed to get laid?"

Ah. It clicked together for Lucas. Mitch had been talking about other issues, issues he couldn't or wouldn't share with anyone else. Hence Kat took it to be something else!

Lucas laughed now, letting his guard back down. He thought she might have figured out who he really was.

"The issue I have is something a lot less naughty, I assure you, Alexa. It is more of a trust issue with woman, not a sexual obsession. I don't date because I don't trust a single female."

Now Alexa looked shocked. Her eyes grew wide but a smile finally broke free. Shaking her head now, she put her glass down.

"Oh, thank God! I was a little worried about doing this with you, knowing... thinking you had an issue like that!" Alexa laughed.

"I'm still seeking sex, and lots of it, Alexa, don't fool yourself."

His words had the effect he wished.

She gulped, picking up her glass and taking a long swallow before meeting his gaze. Her eyes grew darker and he knew she was thinking about what they had done earlier.

"I'm not stupid, I know you want sex."

"Not just sex, I want to consume everything you have to offer, Alexa. I want to do things to you that will make you blush for days."

He leaned in now, his lips brushing hers. That was his last coherent thought for the rest of the night.

Lucas woke in the morning alone in his bed. He barely recalled Alexa saying she had to go to work. He lay there for a while, wondering who was paying for her company today. Looking over on the nightstand where he had put her money, he saw it was gone.

He had paid more than any sane man would have for last night. Which had ended up being worth every penny. Lucas couldn't recall a better toss in the sheets. Alexa was the kind of girl a man didn't get over. If he was not in it only for sex, if he was not the man he was, then he would have already lost his heart.

Thank God for small blessings! If there was one thing he wasn't, it was weak. Not even his Alexa could bring him over the hard lines he had drawn. He didn't linger on his choice of thought of Alexa as his. He side-stepped, avoiding it.

He had a lot of work to oversee today. He couldn't spend any more time thinking about the little dancer.

Mitch was having a board meeting with the remaining members left over from his father's days. He and Mitch hoped to buy them off, leaving no one but him as sole shareholder of the company.

His mother had nearly crippled the company after his father's death, and nearly all the board members had stepped down.

Only a handful stayed. Once Lucas came of age he'd worked his butt off to turn the business around. Then his scandal had rocked the company and the board members, still recalling his father's sins, were ready to pull out.

The company wouldn't have lasted long without them then. However, once Lucas had Mitch fake buy him out, the board members stayed while he faded away, running things from the shadows. Now the company was solid, the name clear of the gossip mills. All that was missing was his name on the side of the building, instead of Mitch's.

If the members gave up their holdings, then Mitch would be eased out. The company would become his and he would bring it into the future with his name at last. This all hung on the members giving up their shares.

They were old but he was not willing to wait till they passed away. He wanted to be able to claim what was his. He had put everything he had into this company.

If they didn't give in sooner or later, all his work and living only half a life would be for nothing. He hadn't sacrificed everything just to be in the shadows of something he'd built.

He didn't plan on getting married for love: he would marry at some point because he wanted children of his own. He would make sure his wife understood this. It would be a business deal more than anything else.

Right now he took what pleasure he could with those willing to give it. Under no false promises. Alexa was the perfect woman for this: a no-strings kind of girl, a girl who was used to nothing longer term.

He couldn't date a normal kind of girl. He avoided hooking up with them which was why he stuck to bars and clubs looking for one-night stands. It had worked out perfect so far.

The one and only time he had let a woman in, she went out of her way to ruin him after he turned her down.

Lucas couldn't allow anything like that to happen again. Not with things so close to being finished. Mitch would not want to be the fake face of his company for ever. He had plans of his own.

The great thing about finding Alexa was now he had something to split his thinking over. He could switch to her when work became too much. And vice versa.

His office phone rang; it was Mitch. The board members wanted to think things over. Lucas had expected this, so he was not restless in waiting it out.

The next three weeks flew by. He spent almost every night with Alexa. He had a hunger for her he couldn't satisfy. No matter how he tried to fill it, come the night he needed to have her in his bed.

It was alarming, but the fact she was there because he paid her kept him from fully worrying about it. When he'd had enough, he would walk away.

ALEXA

Alexa was home for once, waking in her own bed. Lucas hadn't called for her the night before and she was kind of glad.

As much fun as she was having posing as his so-called PIMP girl, she was in sore need of putting some extra hours in at the studio. Thanks to all the time spent between work at the office and with Lucas, she had fallen behind with ballet classes.

Today she was putting in a full day and then some extra time dancing with L.B.C for the performance of *The Sleeping Beauty*.

Their lead had injured her leg, and they needed a fill in. Alexa was a little bustier than they liked, but she was the right size in everything else.

If she didn't needed the extra work, she would have said no. She had not danced for any troupes since she'd received some negative comments on her body. She was not the skinny frame most ballet companies favored and they made sure she knew that.

Alexa took a quick shower, then drove to the studio. She passed the whole day in classes on teaching the various levels from pre-ballet through level five. She felt worn out. The day wasn't over yet, however, as she needed to make it to rehearsal for the show.

The lead male dancer was from Russia taking a term here to earn extra credits. He was only sixteen but already very talented.

They didn't finish up till after midnight. Alexa was dead on her feet and she had to get up early for work in the morning! Once home she unwound by watching a movie, and fell asleep in the living room.

Laughing woke her up. It was Kat was coming in the door, talking on her cell phone. Alexa yawned and checked the time: 4am. She would have to wake up in an hour! Ugh. She might as well stay up now.

"Oh, sorry babe, did I wake you up?" Kat asked.

"Yeah, but it's fine. I need to leave for work soon anyway."

"Still punching the clock at that office job?"

"I need that job, Kat," Alexa pointed out.

"You have a job – two jobs, in fact – and if you count the office gig, three."

"Lucas isn't a job. Not really."

"No? You must have made more with Lucas than you have in a year at your cubicle."

Alexa paused. She had actually already made more money in the last three weeks than her office job could even dream of paying her in two years! Why was she still bothering with it?

Because this thing with Lucas could end anytime and then she would be without income. She didn't want to waste what she had made in her immoral side job on normal living when she was saving for her school.

She explained this to Kat with a sigh.

"Babe, Lucas is hardly close to being done with you. Besides, you can easily find another job, a better one. You don't need to work so hard for so little when you're bringing in the bank you are," Kat told her.

"I would feel horrible giving up my normal job to be a hooker for Lucas, waiting for him to get over his crazy need to fuck me."

"Alexa, think of it as a temping job, except you spend your office hours in bed instead of in a box with a computer."

"I guess I could put in more hours for school if I quit," Alexa mused.

"Yep, you could! And you could sleep in as long as you liked!"

That was the last nail in the coffin for her office job. She did sleep in, and when she woke up she called to tell them she was not coming back. It felt good.

For all of about five minutes. Then the fact she was now solely pimping herself out to Lucas for a living started to work its way into her head, along with the guilt.

Now she could really call herself a PIMP girl, except she wasn't really one – she was just a woman getting paid a lot of money to have sex with a man.

Maybe she was over-thinking things, but she refused to deposit the money into her bank. Getting paid for sex was illegal, and she wasn't about to leave a trail of evidence in the form of cold hard cash.

Keeping the money out of her bank and stuffed in her wardrobe made it less real and kept her from addressing the truth of what she was.

A whore. She didn't like the word. One, it was horrible, and two, she would be freely calling her best friend in the world one too.

Still, how she could look at Kat and not see a whore yet look in the mirror and see it stamped on her forehead in big red letters was beyond her!

Alexa had to take a dozen deep breaths and force herself to recall she was doing this with only one man. A man she would have slept with anyway. She was not going to ever tell a soul outside of Kat what she had done. It would hurt her professional career if it got out she was hooking, no matter the crazy story behind how it came to be.

To make herself feel better, Alexa started to job hunt. She put in applications all over the city. Once she had another legit job, she was sure she would feel less bad about doing what she was doing.

And Lucas hadn't called her, again. Maybe he had gotten over her already. Kat was likely wrong about him not losing interest anytime soon.

The next morning her cell had a missed call from Lucas. *Okay, maybe Kat is right after all,* Alexa thought as she listened to the message. He wanted her to pack for two nights.

 He was going to take her somewhere. Alexa called him back but only got his voice mail. She left him a brief message, asking what she should pack.

He texted her four words: *Dress for hot weather.*

Alexa stared at the four words. Not much to go on, seeing how southern California was hot. She did her best to pack what she thought she would need.

Swimsuit, summer dress, sandals, and whatever else she could fit under the heading 'summer wear'.

Lucas sent a town car to pick her up. Alexa set in the back, the leather seat freezing cold from the air. Goose bumps popped up on her skin. Rubbing her arms she wondered exactly what Lucas had planned.

If things were normal for them, this would be utterly romantic. The kind of thing a girl wished her man would do for her. Things, however, were anything but normal between Lucas and herself.

Pretend it's normal, she told herself.

Yeah, sure! If it was only that easy to forget we are doing this for money! Her inner voice replied.

It was a bad, bad idea to forget the firm line they had in place. Still, Alexa knew if she wanted to get through this without feeling like a tramp, it might be the only way. She didn't have to fall in love – she just had to act like they were dating, and forget the money part.

"Okay," Alexa whispered as the town car pulled up in front of Sunset Resort.

She had only her suitcase of clothes and a smaller bag of toiletries. When the driver offered to help, she declined. Her belly did the whole butterfly thing it always did before seeing Lucas.

When she knocked and Lucas opened the door, her mind was firmly in line with playing along with this being a normal relationship and the tension and guilt slipped away. Lucas was dressed in jeans and a black tank top. He looked damn good.

Alexa licked her lips. The man was hot, and she couldn't get over how handsome he was. Sighing, she followed him into the living room. He offered a glass of tea. It was the first time they'd had something non-alcoholic.

"You look amazing," Lucas said, kissing her forehead.

Alexa blinked, stunned for a moment. This was very much a move a man who was dating a woman would make, not a man who was paying for her company. Lucas never normally did anything outside of the mold of paying costumer.

Yet his simple easy kiss to her forehead did not come into that category. Lucas didn't seem to notice or care if he crossed that line.

 Alexa wondered if he too was forgetting the money part to better enjoy their two-day getaway. She would never know for sure, though, because she refused to bring the issue up.

"Did you pack for two days of sunshine?" Lucas asked.

He was leaning on the island in the kitchen.

"Yes, I packed for hot weather, like you said."

"Good. I'll tell you where we are going once we are in the air." Lucas gave her a goofy little half smile.

It took a short time for Lucas to get this things together and for the town car to once more show up out front.

They drove to a little airstrip where Lucas had his own plane. Alexa wondered exactly how rich he was. Clearly he was very wealthy.

Once the plane was in the air, Lucas did as he promised and told her where they would be spending their two days.

"Puerto Vallarta, Mexico."

"We're going to Mexico?"

"Not just Mexico, Alexa, the best place in Mexico," Lucas clarified.

Alexa smiled, giving him a nod: she didn't really have anything to say. She would spend two days in Mexico, on the beach and in bed with Lucas. It was a perfect getaway for a couple. Sighing, she leaned her head on the small window, watching the sparkle of the blue water below.

"Alexa?" Lucas's smooth voice carried to her over the hum of the engine.

"Um?"

"If you're going to rest your head on something, it should be me."

Lucas put his arms around her, tugging her on to his chest.

"Thanks."

"Now, why don't you catch a cat nap before we land. You'll need your rest." Lucas's voice was a husky murmur at her ear.

Alexa felt a shiver of raw desire wash over her. This really was going to be a good weekend! She didn't think she was sleepy but next thing she knew she was being gently shaken awake by Lucas when their plane landed.

"That was rather quick," Alexa said, with a yawn.

"A little under four hours of flying," Lucas told her.

They got off the plane and took a taxi to their hotel. It was a shining gem next to the aquamarine-colored sea. Their room was a villa right on the water: a pool off to one side enclosed in marble blocked off a small part of the ocean, just for them.

"Wow, this is amazing!" Alexa told Lucas.

She looked around their suite. It was more of a small studio apartment.

"I say we should grab some dinner on the deck then check out the water," Lucas was saying as he put their bags in the back bedroom.

"Good, because I am starving!" Her stomach made a loud sound in agreement.

Dinner was brought to them. It was a mix of spicy chicken on a bed of lettuce and a side of rice. The flavor was so tasty Alexa was nearly licking her plate clean!

A blended drink with salt around the rim of the glass helped wash the food down. It also washed away her worries and she felt relaxed. Alexa smiled as she sipped the last of her drink, watching the sky turn a bright pink over the water.

"Go get your suit on," Lucas called from inside.

Alexa would have been happy to sit here and stare at the water. However, she was looking forward to getting in it too. She had never seen water so blue!

Looking through her bag in the bathroom, she tried to make up her mind which bathing suit to wear. After thinking it over, she went with her bright peach two-piece.

Lucas was busy going through his bag on the bed when she came out. He stopped, his eyes running over her from head to toe before coming back to her breasts, where they stayed a little longer than they should have.

"I am almost tempted to skip swimming!" Lucas grinned.

"Well, you would have to catch me first!" Alexa laughed as she darted out the door.

She could hear Lucas coming after her, the sound of his feet echoing through the villa. Alexa threw herself out the sliding door leading to the sea pool. It was deep enough to dive into and she sprung off the board, hitting the water with a large splash.

The pool was open water below the marble rim, so she went under it, surfacing on the other side of their pool. Lucas was standing on the dock watching her, his hard body on full display in nothing but his board shorts.

"Aren't you coming? This was your idea after all!" Alexa called to him.

Lucas didn't bother going for the pool. He walked out along the marble edging and dove right into the open water. Alexa felt his hand wrap around her ankle and tug. Her head went under. Kicking free, Alexa headed toward the front of the villa.

They chased one another for a while before the need to touch grew too enticing to ignore any longer. Alexa wanted to taste the salt on his skin from the ocean. So when he pulled her into him, she stole a kiss to his throat, running her tongue over the water droplets. He let out a groan, pulling her head back so he could look into her eyes. Those warm brown eyes of his bore into her, making her hot deep inside.

"Have you ever made love in the water, Alexa?" Luca asked, his gaze still pinning hers.

"No."

"Then I am about to change that."

Lucas brought his lips down on hers, in a slow soft kiss. His hands wrapped around her, holding her to him. Alexa wasn't sure how they stayed above the water, nor did she care. Lucas was moving his mouth from her lips, to her neck, to the base of her collar bone.

"You test like paradise," Lucas whispered.

Alexa only sigh as his mouth kissed the flesh of one breast above her swimming top. He moved his head to the other. His hands came to cup her buttocks, moving her heat over his hardness.

Lucas kept up his kisses and his caressing till she was ready to lose her mind. He pulled back and she saw he was able to touch the bottom and this was why they hadn't gone under. He lifted her on to the deck, before hauling himself up as well.

"I thought we were going to do this in the water?" Alexa asked out of breath.

"And so we will, but not with others watching... unless you're into that?" Lucas asked with a lift of his eyebrow.

Alexa looked behind him out on the water and saw a small boat about twenty feet away. Everyone on deck was looking at them.

"Oh my God!" Alexa gasped.

"I didn't think you would want to," Lucas grinned.

"We can head up to the bar for a bit and finish this in the dark of night, or we can go to the bedroom?" Lucas was giving her a choice.

Lucas was not acting like the normal I-paid-for-causal-sex guy she was used too. Was there something more going on now? Alexa wanted him but she liked this new vibe they had going. He had given her a choice, after all.

"We can check out the bar before we finish this."

"After you." Lucas waved his hands toward their room.

Alexa changed out of her bathing suit and into a little black lace dress. After brushing her hair out, she put it up in a messy bun. Applying light make-up and pink lip gloss, she was ready.

Lucas had put on tan slacks and a white button-down dress shirt. His hair was still wet, giving him a devilish appearance. Alexa wanted to push him back on the bed and run her fingers through his 'fuck me' hair.

"You have to stop looking at me like that, really Alexa, else I swear I'm going to rip your clothes off and not care who watches," Lucas said in a hard whisper.

"Sorry, I can't help myself." Alexa gave a bat of her lashes.

"Don't say I didn't warn you." Lucas took her hand and they headed up the wooden walkway to the main part of the beach-front hotel.

A fancy little bar was set up at the water's edge, with plush sofas and chairs and a large dance floor. The place was full. Lucas got them a spot and put in their drink orders. Alexa waited for him at the bar.

"Is that your boyfriend?"

Alexa turned to see a well-dressed woman in dark Chanel sunglasses. She gave her a smile, showing perfect white teeth.

"We're dating," Alexa told her, not wanting to label Lucas as her boyfriend.

"Ah, so nothing serious then?" The woman's long, well-manicured finger was circling the rim of her glass.

"I'm not sure yet, maybe." Alexa gave the woman a big smile.

"Lucky girl," the woman replied in a breathy voice.

"Yep."

Alexa turned her back on the elegant cougar who seemed to want to pounce on Lucas. Really! Not only was she drooling over him, but she was asking his date all the juicy details!

"Come on beautiful, we've got a table." Lucas was suddenly right beside her.

"Don't look, but the woman next to me wants to jump on your bones!" Alexa whispered in his ear on their way to their table.

"Really?" Lucas turned to look back. "Not sure that *is* a woman, babe," he chuckled.

"What?" Alexa turned too and saw a man with dreads setting where the woman had been. "Huh? She must have left." Alexa shrugged.

"No matter, there's only one woman here I'm going to bone." Lucas placed a kiss to her hand.

After a few drinks they found themselves on the dance floor. It was like their first meeting all over again, except now they knew what would come.

Two days were really too short. Lucas packed so much into those days but it still came to an end. He did make love to her in the water like he promised. As well as on their deck and in the villa. Even on the boat they rented too. The whole weekend his loving was much more boyfriend then paying customer!

He drove her back to her house after they got home. Kissing her goodbye, he said he would call her later. It was just an act and Alexa knew she was playing this as a normal thing, but all she could think about were his smoldering brown eyes and his sexy smile.

LUCAS

Lucas stood in front of the mirror looking at the suntanned, goofily-grinning man and wondered who the hell he was. Lucas Kane never looked this happy, never grinned like a schoolboy. Why was he now?

Easy, one word: Alexa. The woman had gotten under his skin, and while he knew he was blurring the lines, Lucas didn't give a damn. He wanted to have a normal connection with the opposite sex for once. Not just sexual, but something more.

Alexa was easy to be with. Her looks made him wild in the sack but her wit kept him from seeing her as only a girl he banged. He'd been playing the boyfriend with her all weekend long and he didn't even feel ashamed of himself for it.

He should be pissed he let it happen but he couldn't bring himself to care. Lucas knew deep down he was letting himself get carried away for the sake of feeling a connection, seeing her as more than great sex.

The lines may be blurry but they still held true. She was a hired amusement and nothing more. Even if she was smart and sexy and funny, Alexa was a causal pastime.

Mitch had been calling him non-stop since he got back the night before, but Lucas wanted to bask in the feeling of bliss he was still reeling in. Now, however, he had to call and see what news his friend had – good or bad.

Mitch answered on the first ring. And he was pissed Lucas had not answered his calls or phoned back sooner. Once Lucas got him to stop babbling about that, he was able to get to the reason he had been calling in the first place.

"Dammit, Lucas! I only call you when I have something worth saying, and if you hadn't spent the last three days sexing it up in Mexico, you might have been able to stop this before it got out!"

Lucas froze in the middle of shaving. His happy mood died in one heartbeat as he forced himself to ask what he could have stopped.

"Pictures of you and Alexa are showing up all over the fucking place! Rumors running wild about you banging a call girl and about how maybe you stepped into your father's shoes and lost your head for a pretty hooker!" Mitch barked.

"Who posted the pictures, Mitch?" Lucas asked, his voice cool.

"Does it matter?"

"You know it does," Lucas reminded him tightly.

"Yes, all right, it was her," Mitch confirmed.

Lucas felt his blood start to boil. He punched his fist into the mirror. It shattered into a spider web of glass and small drips of blood landed in the sink.

The 'her' in question was Cindy Kane, a dark-haired ruthless bitch who ran one of the largest trashy gossip magazines in the world.

And who just happened to be his own mother! Lucas didn't think of her as a mother. The cool distant woman had never mothered him: she had ruined everything in his life.

His father had fallen for her and he had let her take apart his empire. Up to the day he died he had been blinded by the cold-hearted snake. She was nothing more than a social-climbing whore but she had gotten her claws into the right man.

Not even her son was safe from her evil plots and schemes. Thanks to her he was forced to stay in the shadow of his own company, to live a life so far off the fucking map he didn't know who he was anymore!

Bracing himself, he walked into his bedroom and flipped open his laptop. Clicking it to Google, he typed in his name and held his breath. In less than a second hits came up and the source was his mother's publication, *Tainted Magazine*. He thought grimly how aptly it was named.

He clicked the first link and looked at a picture of himself with Alexa wrapped around him, her mouth on his neck and his face lost in lust. He let loose a chain of cuss words as he read the story below the picture.

"Seems the apple doesn't fall far from the tree." Lucas Kane locks lips and more with high-priced call girl, losing more than his money. Seems class and brains aren't included in this package.

Lucas felt his self-control snap as he dressed. He got into his car and headed for downtown to a tall sleek building new to the LA skyline. *Tainted Magazine*'s headquarters loomed in front of him.

He marched in the front door, which was nothing as impressive as the upper levels. Here on the bottom floor were just the info crunchers putting the massive amount of data *Tainted Magazine* had collected into the proper files.

The next floor was the gateway to his mother's trashy kingdom. Done in dark pinks and bright yellows, the room oozed tacky art. The reception desk stood out in gold-painted wood. A short-haired blonde looked up and smiled.

"Can I help you?"

"Yes, I'm here to see Cindy," Lucas growled.

The girl smiled and clicked a button, and he heard his mother's wispy voice.

"What is it?"

"You have a very good looking man here to see you." The blonde gave him another smile.

"Buzz him in."

"All right, you heard her. What business do you have with Cindy today?" the blonde asked, trying to make ideal chit-chat.

"I am going to wring her fucking neck," Lucas growled.

The blonde looked worried but Lucas didn't give her time to think it over as he stormed into his mother's office.

True to her nature, Cindy Kane didn't even blink as Lucas placed his hands on her desk and leaned in, with murder in his eyes.

"Hello, Lucas."

"You've got some fucking nerve! What did I tell you about running your trash on me?" Lucas's voice was full of rage.

Cindy just gave a cold smile, tapping her nails on her smooth cheek as she stared at him, unafraid and unconcerned.

"I do recall you said something along the lines of how you would bury me and everything I own under enough legal shit that I wouldn't see daylight till I was too old to walk."

"I am going to tell you this only once. Retract your fucking smut story and forget my name or I am going to spread a little gossip of my own!"

Cindy laughed. Her light grey eyes danced with malicious humor as she looked at her son. Cocking her head to the side, she studied him.

"You know Lucas, if you could take me down, you would have done it. You hate everything about me, and I know you. You wouldn't hold back if you had anything. And what gossip would you spread about me? No one is going to touch a story with my name in it unless I have agreed to it. I own this town Lucas."

"I don't care what gossip you spread or share as long as I'm not linked to it! I don't give a damn about the other sleaze you spread around. You hardly own this city and I will share your past with all of Los Angeles if you don't comply with my wishes."

Now a little fear ran through those blues eyes as Cindy wondered if Lucas really could do what he promised. Her hand froze in its tapping for a moment before she got up and walked to the window looking over downtown.

"I can't stop other people from running stories about you. You think I am the only one who's got info on you and your little whore?"

"Don't call her that, not when you have no room to talk," Lucas warned her.

"Whatever. I don't care about your little pastimes, Lucas, but others do, and they may still recall your way with women from a few years ago. I am merely one source in the gossip mills. Your little dealings are running through the channels as we speak. Do you plan to bully them all?"

Lucas took a deep breath. His head was pounding, and he knew he couldn't get a choke hold on all the gutter press. Yet he knew Cindy Kane had started this latest smear on him, and had leaked it, and while she may now keep it from her own columns, she wouldn't stop it from reaching other magazine editors in town.

"I'm telling you, if you run, write or share anything about my personal life with anyone, I will not hold back the shit I have on you. If you think it's nothing to worry about, just know it's not mere gossip I'll share!"

Lucas's tone was hard but he kept his voice low and watched the look of panic that finally swept across her face.

"I've done my homework, and I have more dirt on you than you could dream of. If I see or hear one more thing that ties back to you and this shithole, I will release it to the world! You can be on the cover of your own gossip magazine!"

Lucas turned and walked away before he did something he would regret. Like slapping his own mother senseless. He slammed the door hard enough to shake a painting off the wall. It landed on the marble floor with a thud.

The blonde didn't look at him as he exited. She kept her eyes lowered. *Smart chit*, Lucas thought grimly as he made his way out of the building and to his car.

He was praying the little bit of information that had slipped out about him and Alexa would not make it any farther then it had already.

He could only wait and see if Alexa read the article. If she saw herself smeared in the tabloids, would she want to keep sharing a bed with him? She didn't seem like the girl who would want the whole world to know about her life.

Mitch called him as he was driving to his office. He picked up this time and he was slightly worried what news he had to share now.

"Did you go see her?" Mitch asked.

"Yes, and I think she got the point."

"She's not the brightest, Lucas. You've warned her before."

"I think she thought I was joking before, but now she knows I'm not. What else got out?"

"Nothing about the business is linked to you. She doesn't know I run the company only in appearance – that's still under wraps. As for the board members, none of them read anything like *Tainted Mag* and it hasn't gone farther than that," Mitch assured him.

"Good, so we are still on track. Call me once the board has made its mind up." Lucas ended the call.

He needed to clear his head and work the anger out of his body. He headed to his gym. He needed to get in the ring with someone.

Most of the guys knew to avoid him when he came in wanting a fight. Lucky for him there was new blood there today. It didn't go well for him and Lucas was sure afterwards that he'd lost one more person to spar with in future.

Feeling in control once more, he had only one other thing he wanted to do: Alexa. He called her up. She answered, sounding a little sleepy.

"I want to see you today," Lucas told her.

"Okay, it will have to be late. I have dance till ten pm."

"I'll see you around ten-thirty."

Lucas wanted to have dinner waiting for her. He could cook two things well – chicken, and pasta. So he made chicken pasta.

Everything was set and when he heard her knock on the door, his gut tightened. He was giddy like a teenager as he opened the door for her.

"Hey," she said in greeting.

She was dressed in a green t-shirt and blue jeans, her dark blonde hair in a ponytail. She looked damn cute. Lucas had to kiss her. He drew her in, taking her lips in a short kiss.

Alexa had a dreamy look on her face when he pulled away. He smiled. He liked to see the effect of his kisses and his touches.

"I made dinner."

"You cooked for me?" She seemed surprised.

He laughed, seeing her expression. Lucas knew he was crossing those lines again: he was making this a date thing, not an I-paid-you-for-sex thing.

"I did. Come on in, I promise it's good."

Alexa followed him into the dining room. He pulled out her chair and poured her a glass of wine.

"This is really nice, Lucas."

"You deserve nice things," Lucas smiled.

"This might sound crazy, but I have never had a guy cook for me before." She blushed a little now.

"I can't understand what kind of loser you find, Alexa, if none of them have cooked for you or made love to you in the water. You should stick with me."

"Lucas, what is this?" she asked, looking at him.

What indeed, he thought. He didn't know what he was saying. Was it the idea of what Alexa could be? A person to share his life, not just his bed? Was he getting too old for hooking up? Or was Alexa herself working her way past his defenses?

"I don't know, Alexa. You're right, I should watch what I say," Lucas apologized.

"You confuse me sometimes, and I need to know where we stand. This is all a little tricky."

He got what she meant. Lately he had been crossing the lines of their arrangement and she was worried about the outcome.

"I'm not trying to play with your emotions. It's just so damn hard sometimes not to get carried away in the moment with you." He got up and offered her his hand. "I think I need to be reminded about what this really is." Lucas's voice was husky.

Alexa's eyes went wide but she took his hand and let him pull her toward his bedroom. Lucas removed his shirt before sitting on the edge of his bed.

"Strip for me, Alexa." He was back to being the client now.

She did as he asked. Standing in the middle of his bedroom, she slowly pulled her shirt off over her head. Followed by her bra and then her jeans. Finally she slid off her panties, letting them fall to her feet.

"Now come here," Lucas instructed.

Alexa once more did as he asked and stood between his legs. He ran his hand along her sides. Stopping at her hips he pulled her closer.

He kissed a breast and then he took the nipple into his mouth, sucking. He heard her moan and he moved his head to the next soft, pink nipple. Taking it into his mouth too, he grazed it softly with his teeth. He licked and teased her till she was shivering with desire.

"Taste me, Alexa, take me in your mouth."

Lucas wrapped his fingers around her ponytail and held tight while she took his cock into her mouth. The feeling was sheer heaven and all thoughts about how he should be acting or not be acting faded away.

This was about sex right now. After his day, he just wanted Alexa to drive him over the edge, to lose himself in her soft, willing body.

He let her taste him till he was unable to stand it any longer. He didn't want to come into her mouth. He had so much more he wanted to do with her.

"Now lay down and spread your legs, I want to taste you."

Lucas eased her on to her back and moved down her body till he was between her thighs. He parted her with his fingers, running his tongue over her opening, just tantalizing her at first, and enjoying her intake of breath and the look on her face.

Once he got into kissing her and sucking on her little nub, he stopped watching her reaction – he was too busy loving her.

Lucas was so aroused by the time he made her come, he roughly flipped her over onto her stomach and eased his way into her body. He pulled her up onto her knees and thrust into her harder and faster. He came with a loud shout of her name.

He was spent. He rolled over, tucking her loosely into the crook of his arm and then he fell asleep. Lucas slept like the dead.

When he did wake up, Alexa was gone. He didn't think much of it, she often left if she had work so he showered and headed for the office.

He put together her payment and sent it off to her with his driver. Last night had worked to rid his body and mind of their tension and firm back up the lines between Alexa and himself.

Things were back in order. He spent the day locked in meetings with Mitch so he didn't text or call to check up on Alexa. And since he had a business dinner with Mitch tonight, he decided he would call her tomorrow and plan to have her come stay the night with him.

He was finishing up the last part of his work for the day, when his cell started to ring. He saw it was Mitch. He was likely checking the time for their dinner.

"Dinner is at seven."

"What? No dude, that's not why I am calling. Have you checked out *Tainted Mag*'s newest issue?"

Lucas felt a rumble building in his chest. If Cindy had not followed his orders, he was going to unleash hell on her!

"If she printed another goddamn story on me, I am going..."

Mitch cut him off.

"It's not you, Lucas, it's her, Alexa. She ran a story on Alexa."

Mitch's words hit him.

"Alexa?" Lucas asked in a stupor.

"Yeah, Alexa, and it's not a favorable story."

Lucas was busy hitting keys on his computer, and when the story popped up it came with a large, full color photo of Alexa dancing on the stage and one of her topless with him in Mexico. His heart stopped. The words below the pictures knocked the air from his lungs.

How grace has fallen! The once prim and proper ballerina is selling her body to the elite and rich! Once an upcoming star in the ballet world, Alexa Kelly, who famously stood her ground within the ballet world, promising to start a school of her own to shy away from the unacceptable body demands on a ballerina, is now whoring herself out! Last seen getting it on with unknown billionaire!

Lucas was pissed. He was so upset he could not think straight. *God, what just happened?* Alexa had been a star in the ballet world? She was going to start a school? Something like this could ruin her name! He had no idea she was working on anything like this! He hadn't asked, either.

He knew Cindy was pushing his buttons. She had not said anything about him, only Alexa. Clearly she had enough to know who Alexa was and what was going on between them.

How? This was what Lucas was wondering about now. How did she know about Alexa? This story could blow up, go viral and everyone who knew Alexa would know all her secrets!

There was nothing he could do to stop this. He could only be there for her. He could only help her weather this, and maybe they could spin it that she was his girlfriend? His mind was working overtime.

He dialed her number but it went straight to voice mail. He tried again and left a message for her to call him as soon as possible.

Lucas set off to meet Mitch, leaving his cell phone on, prepared to take the call if and when she did finally call him back.

At the restaurant, Mitch took one look at him and sighed. He pushed a drink at him before taking a sip of his own.

"Man, be glad your name is not linked to this – it's gone national!"

"Alexa shouldn't have her name smeared like this!" Lucas growled at Mitch.

"Easy, man, I agree, but the girl works at a place that hires her out to rich men for dates, so really, what did she except?" Mitch asked reasonably.

Lucas shot him a dark look. He had a point, but this was Alexa, and Lucas didn't like anyone thinking bad things about her.

"Look, dude, it sucks, but you know I'm right," Mitch told him.

"Maybe, but I feel horrible about this."

"Of course you do. You're a decent guy, Lucas, but you didn't force her into anything."

"No, but it's my mother who is smearing her name."

"Yes, but Alexa set herself up for such a risk when she took a job being a PIMP girl." Mitch was a little too cold about this but with reason.

Lucas put aside his guilt over Alexa and got down to business with Mitch. Later he would figure out how to help Alexa fix this situation.

ALEXA

The water was running cold in the shower. Alexa wasn't sure how long it been running at this temperature and she didn't care either!

Her bad night had just became a bad day. She was still reeling over Lucas's crazy switch back to being just-about-sex guy when a picture on the cover of one of Kat's magazines caught her eye.

There on the damn cover she stood posed on stage, and right next to that was her topless in Mexico with Lucas!

Horrified she quickly scanned the story and felt instantly ill. They were labeling her a call girl who had thrown away her life and ambitions to screw the rich and elite!

Her phone started to ding like mad and she quickly turned it off. Still in shock and beyond embarrassed, she had gotten into the shower and was still standing there with freezing water washing over her body.

Nothing about Lucas. Wouldn't they care more about the billionaire instead of some nameless ballet dancer?

Alexa was hard pressed to find a reason why they would be running her personal life on the cover of a gossip magazine? She wasn't anybody. Not yet anyway, and with this kind of publicity, she would never be anyone!

The shower door slid open. Before she could scream, Alexa saw Kat standing there with a towel in her hand.

"Get out. Death by drowning or freezing in a shower is hard to accomplish, girl." Kat offered a weak smile.

"I'm not trying to kill myself, Kat. I may wish the earth would open and swallow me or fire from the sky would consume me, but I would never off myself."

"We need to get to the bottom of this," Kat stated, draping the towel around Alexa's shoulders when she got out.

"How do you suppose we do that? March over to the magazine and demand answers?" Alexa asked.

"No, we are going to meet them at Pot Lobby," Kat announced.

"Meet them? Who?"

"Someone from *Tainted Magazine*, that's who, silly."

Alexa wasn't sure what to say next. Part of her wanted to hide in her room for the rest of her life but another part wanted to bitch slap someone for running such a story! Didn't they know they were messing with people's lives?

"How did you set this up?"

"Easy, doll face. I called and got heated with a staff member who sent me to someone who agreed to meet with the 'ballerina' in question and get her side of the story."

"My side of the story! I don't want to give them more to publish, Kat! I want them to stop running the story of me being a call girl!"

"And we will get them to, and make sure they clear up the fact about you being a call girl. It's the only way to fix this," Kat assured her.

Great. She didn't want to talk about what really was going on between her and Lucas. They hadn't said anything about him and she wanted to keep him out of the limelight too.

Getting dressed turned into an event with Kat there bossing her around.

"You need to look good but not over-sexy. You want to avoid the whole 'sex for money' look as much as possible! But you don't want to look like a loser."

Kat was going on and on as she put together an outfit for Alexa.

Alexa eyed the knee-length black dress and green velvet jacket with an eerie sense of déjà vu. This whole mess had started with Kat picking an outfit for her. She removed her jeans, the ones not fit for redeeming your reputation, so it seemed, and put on the dress and jacket.

"Perfect! You look cute, not slutty!"

Kat didn't give her time to mull over what she was about to walk into. She dragged her sharply out the door and into her Hummer. Alexa let the events unfold, too overwhelmed to stop them.

The Pot Lobby was one of the hottest bars in LA and it was crammed with people. Alexa followed Kat as they weaved through the crowd.

"Oh! There she is!" Kat said, pointing to a woman in white at the bar.

"You're sure?"

"Yes, she told me she would be in white and at the bar."

"Okay, let's go." Alexa shrugged.

"She wants to talk to only you, doll. I'll be right over there." Kat indicated a table in the corner.

Clenching her jaw to keep from screaming, Alexa gave Kat a tight smile and headed up to the woman in white. Alexa took a seat next to her and the woman turned to say hello. Alexa stopped cold. The woman with the lush red mouth pulled back in a winning smile was wearing black Chanel sunglasses!

"You! I know you!" Alexa blurted out.

"So you do recall our little run in," the woman said, with a husky laugh.

"You took those pictures?" Alexa demanded.

"I did. I was following a lead and doing my job. I had no idea who you were. I was merely told you were paid by Mr. Kane to be his escort." She shrugged one dainty shoulder as if it was no big deal.

"Kat told you the truth?"

"Yes, your friend cleared up the little misunderstanding. She works for PIMP and you only went as a double date, unaware of the impression your date was under about you. I get it. It's all a case of mistaken identity. Yet the press doesn't care, and when someone as rich and powerful as Mr. Kane throws you under the newshound bus, what's a girl to do?"

"Wait, who is this Mr. Kane?"

Alexa didn't know a Mr. Kane, did she?

"Lucas Kane? Your billionaire – the one under the wrong impression of his date? You mean to tell me he didn't give you a last name?"

Alexa's head was spinning with all the questions and info flying at her now. Lucas's last name was Kane? He had thrown her under the bus? She wasn't sure what the lady was talking about!

"I'm sorry… what's your name?"

"Cindy," the woman offered.

"Okay, I'm sorry Cindy, I don't follow. What do you mean, Lucas throw me under the bus? He told you to run a story about me?"

Cindy lowered her Chanel sunglasses, showing off a pair of shrewd, grey eyes.

"Let me explain it in a simpler manner for you. Lucas Kane doesn't let his name get smeared. He's had enough bad press to last him a lifetime. So when *Tainted* found out about him paying for sex, we went after the story. We were going to lead with him, and your name was not going to come up. Yet when he saw the mock-up on our website, he freaked out. He demanded we remove it. I'm not sure why, but after making sure we retracted it he felt the need to offer up your story. One he clearly didn't know everything about, but that didn't stop him from spilling his guts about you, Alexa Kelly."

Cindy pushed her sunglasses back into place.

Alexa wasn't breathing anymore. Her heartbeat was accelerating rapidly as her mind flooded with flashbacks of her and Lucas. Of his mouth on hers, his hands, the gentle way he'd kissed her forehead that day. He'd cooked for her, flown her to Mexico and like a fool she had let herself feel for him. It wasn't as if she didn't know what the facts were. He thought she was for sale – her time, her body.

She'd let him think this because she was attracted to him, and what could it hurt?

Her. It ended up hurting her. Not only her, but possibly her career and her reputation as well. And now she was learning he gave a gossip magazine a story to run about her!

"Do you need me to explain it again?" Cindy asked.

Alexa snapped out of her daze, focusing in on the woman in white.

"No, Cindy, thank you. I get the fact Lucas is an asshole. Now, why don't you tell me why you agreed to meet me here? To run another story? To spread more gossip for the trashy tabloid trolls?" Alexa felt the anger shaking her voice.

"No, I want to give you a voice in this. After your friend filled me in on the truth, I knew you had to get your side out. To save your name, Alexa. I can't run anything about Lucas Kane but I know a lot of tabloids that would die for your story. Give me the green light and I'll make sure they paint him as the asshole he is, and clear up the little misunderstanding that half of America, and maybe more, is now reading and believing."

Alexa heard her inner voice telling her to do it. *Clear your name!* Yet, could Lucas truly be that much of a bastard? Could he have sold her out? Alexa still couldn't accept that.

"Cindy, this has been a rough day, and my mind is mush. Can I get back to you with my story?" Alexa needed to speak to Lucas first.

Cindy nodded, her lips pursing into a pout as she dug into her purse and pulled free a card. Handing it over, she got up.

"I understand you need to think before you speak. This is a card I give my journalists: it has all the contact info of where to send your story. When you're ready."

Alexa watched her go. Something about the woman rubbed her the wrong way. Yet she could not overlook all the facts pointing to Lucas behind this all. She wasn't someone to do rash things, not normally. Before she stuck it to Lucas, there had to be no doubt whatsoever that he really did tell them to go after her.

Her cell had been off for nearly twelve hours. Turning it back on she found tons of phone calls and text messages, mostly from Kat. Two were from Lucas and one was from L.B.C Groaning, she decided she would deal with the ballet part after she figured out Lucas's hand in all of this.

Clicking his number she put the phone to her ear and waited. He answered right away.

"Alexa, I was hoping you would call me."

His voice sent shivers down her spine.

He could be the enemy, stop picturing him naked! her inner voice sneered. Reining in her emotions, Alexa got ready to ask the tough questions.

"Lucas, we need to talk."

"I am assuming you saw the story in *Tainted*?" Lucas asked.

"Yes, and I'm not happy about it."

"No, I didn't think you would be. Come over, let's figure things out," Lucas said.

"I'll head over now." Alexa didn't linger on the other end and she hung up. A lump was forming in her throat.

Even if Lucas was not the reason her name was smeared in the papers, he had treated her like an object the night before. While she knew what kind of deal they had, Lucas had never treated her that way before. True, he was all business but nothing close to the cold person he'd been the last time they'd slept together.

She would have to address this too. Not something she was looking forward to. Driving over, her insides kept cramping, her heart rate was bordering on alarming, and all the while the need to have him touch her was growing.

Alexa found herself standing in front of Lucas's flat. Her hand paused a few inches from the door. Somehow she was able to force herself to knock.

Lucas was filling the door frame and her senses much quicker than she wished for. His bare chest greeted her, making her mind wander, sidetracking her. Only for a moment, however. Pushing past him, Alexa stopped in the middle of the room.

"Lucas, I need to know who you are." Alexa turned and waited for him to answer.

Lucas shut the door. Leaning against it he folded his arms and stared her down. Those light gold eyes pinned her.

"You need to know who I am? Alexa, what do you mean exactly by that statement?"

"I mean, I need to know what kind of man you are. What is your last name? What do you do? How do you spend your days? Those things I have no idea about."

"My name you know: Lucas. You want a last name? Fine, it's Kane. I'm Lucas Kane and I run a multi-million dollar company. How I spend my days, well, I think you understand better than most. Now, what does any of this have to do with the issue of you being a tabloid story?" Lucas was growling at her now.

"Lucas, I'm a nobody. I dance. I'm not famous enough for any tabloid to care about. But you are. You're the one who is newsworthy not me, yet it's funny how your name didn't come up, isn't it?" Alexa folded her arms now too, glaring right back into those golden ones.

"A nobody? Did it not say rising star in the ballet world? Clearly you're far from being a nobody. And I don't let my name get smeared in the papers, Alexa. Never." His words were hard and cold.

Goose bumps rushed down her arms. Those sounded close to the same words Cindy had told her he'd said. *Dammit*. Lucas seemed to be shaping into the type of person she feared he might be.

"Never? How do you stop a gossip mag from running stories about you?" Alexa inquired, holding her breath, wanting to know the answer, yet fearing his next words all the same.

"I use any means necessary to keep my name out of their smut press. I am sorry about your name but don't think I'm going to throw myself in front of the bus to save you." Lucas closed the distance between them. "You want to know how you keep your name out of a sleazy magazine, Alexa?" Lucas asked softly.

Alexa didn't say a word; she wasn't sure she could speak.

"You don't work at a place that sells you off to the highest bidder. You don't take up a life on the stage! You keep yourself so far off the fucking grid that even you forget who you are!" Lucas was now right in her face.

"Are you... are you saying this is my fault?" Alexa demanded, finding her voice.

"All I am saying is you chose your life. I didn't make you what you are."

His words stung. If he'd taken a knife to her gut it couldn't have hurt worse.

Alexa could feel the tears gathering but blinked them away. He had just clarified he would do whatever it took to keep his name from being ruined, including damaging hers.

"You're an asshole," Alexa snapped.

She shoved past him, heading for the door, but he grabbed her by the arm and spun her round. Her body made contact with his. She glared up at him.

"I am sorry the truth hurts, Alexa, but this isn't on me," Lucas told her.

"Not on you? Who else should it be on? You think I do this kind of thing regularly? Before you, I had never crossed any moral line!" Alex informed him, pulling her arm loose.

"So, you hadn't been tempted by anyone before me? Well, that still doesn't make it my fault you gave in."

"You're not even sorry, are you?" Alexa asked softly.

Emotions ran over Lucas's face, but only for a moment before it smoothed back out. He reached for her but only managed to get a grip on her purse. The purse hit the floor. Alexa quickly retrieved it then put more space between herself and Lucas.

"I'm not going to apologize for what we shared. I'm not sorry I got you in my bed. Once more, Alexa, I didn't force you into this. You made your choices."

"We shared nothing but meaningless sex, Lucas."

His eyes narrowed and he took a threatening step forward before stopping himself. He looked pissed, yet when he did speak, it was in a cool tone.

"Meaningless sex is what I paid for."

Alexa didn't want to hear any more. He was under the wrong idea and that was her fault. Yet he had sold her out to save his own name. Why did offer her up after he was free and clear? *Because he's a prick*! her inner voice answered.

Clearly he was not the man she thought he was. Ha! She had no idea who he was! He was a stranger to her – a stranger who shared sex with her for money! What kind of man did she think he was going to end up being?

A rich jerk who got what he wanted and didn't feel bad about ruining the life of someone who he considered was beneath him. Alexa knew she had been playing a risky game, forgetting for a while what was really going on between them.

Guilt was her best friend keeping her head on straight, but she gave that up so she could feel better about spending her nights with Lucas. He was right: she had set herself up for this fall! However, she was damned if she would go down alone!

Once she got home she went straight to her laptop and flipped it open. She went to her account which she'd already created on the website whose details had been on the card Cindy had given her. Now a blank white screen blinked at her. Tell her side of the story? Oh, you bet she would! Lucas fucking Kane thought he was untouchable? Not after she got done!

The words poured out of her. Alexa's fingers moved across the keyboard in a flurry of movements, and when she was finished she called Kat in to read it.

"This is brilliant! Man, everyone is going to hate Lucas Kane! You come over funny here as well as pissed!"

"I am pissed, Kat! He did this to me for no good reason! If he thinks he can walk all over me he has another think coming!"

"I feel like this is somehow my fault," Kat confessed, after a moment.

"Kat, don't feel like that! You had no idea he would turn out to be such an ass," Alex told her soothingly.

"Then you don't hate me?" Kat asked.

"No! I love you. I hate Lucas Kane!"

With those words, she clicked the send button. Now her story about Lucas Kane was waiting to come out to the world. Tomorrow she would have to face the L.B.C and her own school and see what could be done about saving her dream.

The next day she sat in the office of L.B.C they had read the original story about her and Lucas, and, like herself, the management there was horrified by the content. They told her she couldn't dance for them if her name was tainted. Pun, thanks to *Tainted Magazine*.

Alexa quickly went over the same story she had sent out the night before and told them they would soon be reading the true events of what occurred between her and Lucas Kane.

"While we're glad to hear it was a misunderstanding, we are risking a lot keeping you on as lead dancer," Thomas, the director, said.

"If you feel it's too high risk, then let me go." Alexa didn't want to dance on the stage anyway. Not like this. She had bigger dreams – her own studio and school she wanted to run.

"If we do, you won't have clocked up enough time for dancing and you'll lose your spot in the program."

Alexa sighed. Of course, she had forgotten what spending so many nights with Lucas had resulted in. She had lost out time in dance, and if she didn't make it up with L.B.C she would be giving up her spot for training with the top teachers in the ballet world.

She needed so many hours a week dancing in order to hold onto that place. She couldn't afford to lose it.

"Please tell me what I need to do." Alexa didn't like them having something to hold over her though.

"We agree you should dance two productions with us. And if the real story behind the mishap does run, we won't take any action to have you removed."

Alexa nodded. What else could she say? If she wanted to hold on to the spot in the program she would need to dance to their tune till her hours were made up. However, she wouldn't be their doormat! She had been one before and Alexa refused to do it again.

"Fair enough, but once my hours are made up I won't be dancing on stage anymore." Alexa shook hands with Thomas and went about putting the whole mess of Lucas behind her.

Or so she thought. By that night her story of Lucas had made it to the news. Kat about beat her black and blue slapping her on the back as the report retold the story on the air.

Her hope that her little story would just grace the eyes of those who most needed to know the truth, and nothing more, had been foolish.

It was like wildfire spreading through the news feeds. Everyone seemed to be talking about the sweet ballerina caught up in the clutches of the evil billionaire and his wicked ways. How he had tried to tarnish her name to save his. Lucas's name was plastered everywhere now.

Alexa found herself wondering how he was reacting to all this before reminding herself she didn't care. She wanted him to face the music, after all.

The fame from the story kept getting in the way of her everyday life. She went from nobody to whore to hero in less than a week!

"I can't even go shopping without reporters stalking me!" Alexa was complaining to Kat one hot summer afternoon three weeks after the story went live.

"You're famous now, love," Kat said, with her normal good humor.

"I don't want to be famous, not like this anyway," Alexa sighed.

"Well, it's a little too late to change your mind now!" Kat reminded her.

Kat was right. She couldn't go back in time. Even if she could, Alexa knew she would have done the same thing. Clearing her name had felt good! And more good things started to happen for her as well.

The program leader called to inform her a New York school run by the second best teacher in the world was offering her a spot to come learn and teach in their program. It was what she had always wanted. While she would have to grace the stage again a few times for them back east, she would be spending most of the time studying teaching methods from some of the top names in ballet. The best of the best from all over the world under one roof!

Alexa didn't have to think too hard. She needed to get away from the craziness in LA caused by her story and she would be living out a lifelong dream. What was there to think about really? She said yes.

Kat helped her pack. Alexa still didn't want to put the money she earned from Lucas in the bank, not till all this blew over. Kat said she would wire her the money once she got settled in.

The next weekend she was flying to New York. Lucas could have LA!

Lucas

Lucas stared at the card on his living room floor. It had slipped out of Alexa's handbag when she'd dropped it. He knew what it was the moment his eyes lit on it. It was the card all his mother's journalists needed – they used it to post their smut online for Cindy to review. Yet now he knew Cindy wasn't running the story, but every other major tabloid and news channel was!

He paid his mother another visit. He was ready for blood, and when he stormed in ready to get it, he found for once his mother was not running anything about him.

One of her employees had gone after a story on him apparently, but the girl didn't know it was her son she was going after. And when Cindy saw the name, she'd passed but the girl had clearly found other means to get her story published. That was what his mother's words had been to explain away how her card had been in Alexa's possession.

"Lucas, she worked for me part-time and was just doing her job. I can't change the fact she was 'working' for you too but I didn't print her story... but someone sure did."

Cindy had turned on the TV to prove her point.

"Alexa worked for you? I thought she worked as a PIMP girl?"

"Lucas, Lucas, Lucas, Have you learned nothing? Women lie, and she worked you over for a story. The girl was never a PIMP girl."

Lucas felt his gut twist. He had let an enemy right into his bed! The fact Alexa had been playing him was boiling his blood. Alexa was so good in bed he really thought she was what she claimed to be. Why had he not put it together sooner?

This explained the story his mother wanted to run about him and how she knew about Alexa. Of course she did! Alexa was working for her! After he questioned his mother, he went and got good and drunk.

He spent a few weeks in a drunken haze, not wanting to think about anything clearly. Mitch finally showed up to knock some sense into him. The board members had signed off, giving everything over to Mitch. The old tycoons didn't know anything about the tech protection company. They stayed because of what the company used to be.

So now the company was all his, except, thanks to Alexa, he couldn't step up. Not with all the bad press surrounding his name. He was finally free to show the world K-Enterprise was his company – his sweat and blood had built it – but thanks to another lying female he would have to remain in the shadows. Mitch tried to convince him to still step forward.

"Lucas, the company is sound. I don't think some bad press is going to ruin you and all you have built," Mitch pointed out.

"You don't know her. Mitch. I'm sure once Cindy learns I've rebuilt what was once my father's she will do everything she can to take it down."

"I don't get how a mother could do such a thing to her son. Your mother is a twisted bitch."

Lucas didn't take offense to his mother being bad-mouthed. He knew all too well she was screwy in the head.

"Exactly why I can't link my name and face to K-Enterprise, not yet."

"Dammit Lucas, this brooding-behind-the-scenes-billionaire act is getting old," Mitch muttered.

Lucas let out a harsh laugh at Mitch's complaint. He too was sick of pulling the strings from his office behind closed doors.

"I am over the whole secret identity thing, I assure you. But I can't risk ruining everything I've worked for," Lucas pointed out.

"I hear you, but you're nowhere near billionaire status, close but not there yet!" Mitch snorted.

"True. I'm not quite that rich. Even though Alexa seems to think so." Lucas flinched just from saying her name. He had avoided all things Alexa but couldn't hold back that one.

"The whole world now thinks you're a kinky version of Bruce Wayne!"

"They're clearly lacking the facts then," Lucas said.

"You really do have miserable luck when it comes to women."

"And I don't need you to point it out, even if it's true," Lucas snapped.

"Since you're in one of those moods, I'm going to take myself off to do some fake business shit why you stay here and lick your wounds. Just don't stay locked up in here moping like a teenage girl for much longer!" Mitch said before he headed out.

Lucas didn't plan to stay locked inside his house. No, he planned to turn the tables on his little spy. Alexa didn't know the resources he had at his fingertips to make her life a living nightmare! She may have saved face with the world, but Lucas knew other ways to get even.

He wasn't the kind to turn the other cheek, as the saying went. If she thought he would just hang his head and ride it out like he did the last time, she was about to learn otherwise. Lucas had money to spare. He hired a private investigator to dig up all he could on Alexa Kelly. To watch her every move. Lucas knew when she left for New York.

After a few weeks, he knew Kat was sending her money every month. He had paid Alexa a very large amount during the time they spent together. She didn't need Kat's money. With a little help from Mitch, who did some digging around at Kat's, he found out what was going on.

Alexa had left the money at Kat's to send on once she got settled. Of course Kat wasn't about to tell anything to Mitch willingly, but he'd found it all laid out in text messages between her and Alexa when he'd 'borrowed' Kat's cell.

 Lucas planned to get the money back. It was under false pretenses he'd paid her in the first place. Alexa wouldn't be getting her next monthly installment. It took little effort for him to get Kat's money transfer to her intercepted.

He left a note in the dress drawer, addressed to Kat herself. It was straight to the point.

Dear Kat,

Please inform Alexa I am taking back my payments. I am sure she will understand the reason why. Feel free to call the cops to report the money stolen, but just be ready state where it originally came from. No? I didn't think so. Tell Alexa she can earn it back... And I am sure she knows how... I'll be in touch.

LK

He wasn't finished with her yet. Lucas planned to repay her in kind. She set him up for the fall and now he was going to walk her into a scandal all her own. First he would force her into a tight spot till she had no options left but to take his money, and the only way Alexa would get her hands on it was if she put hers on him.

A smile spread over his face. It was ironic, the turn she would have to take. Without the money she had no income. Alexa wasn't working for *Tainted* either.

He dug into that too. Seemed Alexa truly had worked for his mother with that story. It was stupid to think it was just a lie. Lucas didn't know why he was holding out for another explanation, but he had been.

Now all that was left was to kick back and wait. He gave it month before Alexa would be forced to contact him. As the days rolled into weeks Lucas waited, but when the month came and went he started to second guess himself. Seemed Alexa had more pride than he originally thought.

It was a bright Sunday morning when he finally got the answer to the reason she never called. Lucas Kane was once more in the headlines. This time a picture of the note he had left at Kat's was spread on the cover of *US Today*.

Seems bad boys don't give up that easily. Naughty billionaire sends demands once more for a certain ballerina! Learn more about Lucas Kane's kinky sex addictions!

"Shit!" Lucas swore, slamming his laptop closed.

Damn! He really had no idea who Alexa was! He hadn't figured she would react in this manner! He had taken her lifeline, left her helpless. Hadn't he? Clearly she wasn't going to turn to him.

Surprisingly *Tainted* hadn't published anything about the bestselling story to rock the gossip columns. This made him wonder what hand his dear mother had in it all. No way she didn't have her hands dirty!

Lucas knew there had to be a way to reach Alexa to affect her, to crush her dreams and hopes. To make her pay for what she had done. This was personal now, unlike before with the woman who'd spent one night with him and brought his world crashing down with lies and gossip. Before he had only cared about his name being trampled on.

Now his heart had been. Lucas didn't like the thought. He didn't want to think how close he had come to giving himself fully to Alexa. He had fallen for her, lost himself in those eyes.

There was more than sex between them. He cared, had cared, but now he didn't, or so he told himself. Now it was all about getting even. Lucas spent hours brainstorming ways to break Alexa far enough that she would have to submit to him.

Nothing was coming to him. Lucas was forced to put aside his revenge plots for the night. It was Mitch's birthday and he was spending it with his friend getting plastered. Hopefully thoughts of Alexa would fade away for a while.

All was going well till Mitch brought up the newest gossip about him spreading through the city. He was glad to be halfway drunk so he didn't have to think too hard about it.

"I think you should give up hunting this chick down. She is too fucking cunning for even you, Lucas. I hate to say it."

"It was a stupid move on my part, but I won't make the same mistake next time," Lucas promised.

Mitch groaned and rolled his eyes before tossing another shot back. Lucas knew he should let it go but he couldn't.

"I don't think you can win this war. I mean, what can you do to her? You took her money, she didn't care, and you can't beat her in the press, not now. You're screwed."

Mitch handed him a shot.

"You would have to own the fucking ballet school or something to mess up her life. You don't. Let it go man, just let it go."

Mitch slapped him on the back before making his way onto the dance floor Lucas shrugged, just far enough gone not to give a rat's ass.

Downing his shot, he leaned back on the plush chair, closing his eyes. Mitch's words rolled through his mind. Own the fucking ballet school. Own the.... Damn, he had it!

ALEXA

New York had been fun. Yet Alexa was glad to be back in sunny California. She didn't get to finish more than one term in the Big Apple, but she had done enough to earn some credit for her name.

When she first learned Lucas had intercepted the money, she'd panicked. She had nothing else! Then, when Kat sent her a photo of the note he'd left behind, she got good and mad. How dare he try to force her into becoming his plaything again?

Sending the picture and a short story to all the gossip magazine had been Kat's idea. It was a great one! They all wanted to run it, but she gave it to the highest bidder and the pay equaled a night with Lucas.

Lucas Kane was gold to the gossip mags. A hot rich guy with issues and lots of dirty secrets? Sold! It was getting easier not to worry about how this was affecting Lucas: after all, he seemed to not care what happened to her.

Things for her were looking up. While she had to give up New Your after just a short stay she did get into something better here at home. A new school was opening up and being run by one of the newest and best teachers in ballet history.

When they asked for her to join them, she had squealed like a five-year-old at Disneyland and accepted without a second thought. There was a small initial tuition payment, but after that her hours spent in the school went towards her lessons so she didn't have to pay anything else. Getting a part-time job would meet the bills.

Alexa was looking forward to forgetting Lucas and the press stories. All she wanted was to get back to finishing up her schooling so she could open her own studio. Which did leave her with finding a way to pay for a space.

 With Lucas's money gone, she didn't have any funds to spare on buying a space or putting down for renting one.

Determined not to stress over something she wouldn't be able to do anyway for a few years, she pushed it back down into the pit with all her other worries and fears.

Alexa was looking for a part-time job. She sat down at her and Kat's favorite coffee shop poring over the 'help wanted' ads one afternoon.

"You could always apply to work for real at PIMP," Kat suggested.

"Yeah, no thank you! Not that I would be ashamed or anything, but after the fake run with it I'm thinking it is best to avoid anything too risky."

Kat just smiled before going back to sipping her iced coffee. Alexa was now always fearful of what the press would do if she got mixed up in anything closely related to being naughty. She had dodged a bullet first go around, but she didn't want to add fuel to the fire.

"I'm sorry, I know I'm being nosey, but if you're looking for work, my dear Alexa, why not come work for me?" a familiar raspy voice asked from behind her.

Turning around she saw Cindy in a floral sundress and her famous sunglasses. She was sitting at the table right behind her and Kat.

"Work for *Tainted*?" Alexa asked

"Why not? You will make better pay then anything you will find in those ads, I promise you that."

"I'm not writing anything more about Lucas Kane," Alexa warned, in case she wanted her for that very reason.

"No, I wouldn't think of it. I want you to cover my fashion trends section," Cindy confirmed.

"I have school and it comes first, so I would need to have flexible hours."

"Then it's perfect fit because you can write any place, any time, as long as you meet the printing deadline," Cindy confirmed.

"Okay, thanks. I guess I'll give it a try," Alexa nodded.

After an awkward handshake, Alexa agreed to come to *Tainted*'s offices to sign the paperwork and get everything set up. Things were falling into place so easily, it was hard for her to believe it was all working out!

It wasn't long before she had a routine down. Monday through Friday she spent clocking hours at the new studio, and on the weekends she went to work on her column for *Tainted*, making sure it was turned in on Sunday night so it was ready for Monday's press run.

Alexa was looking forward to this weekend. She was covering a runway show in Hollywood for work, and her plus one was Kat. They'd already been shopping for new dresses to wear. Kat had gotten a tight lacy red number. Alexa ended up with a classic little black dress with an open back all the way down to just above her buttocks.

It was a great start to a fabulous evening, and as the party got going after the show, Alexa found she was having a good time. There was a long queue at the bar, so leaving Kat to hold their table she went to get the drinks.

"Fancy running into you here... Alexa." The husky voice shot right through her body.

Turning around, she faced Lucas's broad chest in a navy blue dress shirt. Looking up to his face, she wished she hadn't bothered. A clear look of hate pinned her down. Alexa's first reaction was to turn around and flee.

"What, no words from the famous Alexa Kelly? Not for the man she has so much to say about?" Lucas taunted.

"You asked for it," Alexa hissed.

"Really? I asked you to lie to me and pretend to be someone you weren't, and then use me to sell stories?" Lucas growled.

"Once more, Mr. Kane, you started it. I just happen to give as good, as I get!"

"Yes, I remember that... fondly," Lucas leaned in to whisper near her ear.

"Asshole!" Alexa breathed, backing up.

"You have no idea."

"Don't I?" Alexa challenged.

"Please don't give me a sob story about how I wronged you, Alexa. You may not be a whore but you're far from being the innocent you play! You work for a trashy gossip magazine not exactly known for its honor!" Lucas told her.

"I don't cover the gossip column, Lucas, I cover the fashion! Not that it's any of your damn business!"

Alexa was ready to make her exit, but Lucas's big hand wrapping around her arm stopped her.

"Let go!" she demanded, eyeing the crowd. People had stopped to watch them.

Lucas pulled her into his arms, bringing his face close to hers. She knew he was going to kiss her, here in the bar with everyone watching. His lips crushed into hers, stealing her mouth in a hard kiss.

It was over quickly, too quickly for her, yet she still wiped her mouth for good effect and gave Lucas a disgusted look.

"There now, they have something to talk about!" Lucas's words sank in as he turned and walked away.

Alexa hadn't missed the flash of cameras when they were kissing. Meaning someone was getting a story! Here she was, bashing the man in question in the press and then kissing him openly in a bar. It wouldn't matter it was a stolen kiss, the press would run it however they liked!

Groaning she forgot about the damn drinks. Heading for Kat, she pulled her out of the party, ignoring her protest.

"What's the matter with you?" Kat asked, after being dragged outside.

"We're leaving."

"Leaving, why? It was just getting good in there!"

"That's likely the reason Lucas Kane was there too!" Alexa spat.

"Lucas is here? You saw him?"

"I did more than see him, he talked to me… and then he kissed me! Kissed me because he wanted the gossip hunters in there with cameras to catch me kissing him!"

"Shit! Alexa, you need to avoid Lucas – like the plague!"

"No kidding! It's not like I didn't try but Lucas makes it hard to walk away," Alexa muttered.

"He is fine," agreed Kat.

Rolling her eyes, Alexa got in Kat's car. He was fine, but it wasn't the reason she hadn't got away. He had a grip like steel! Rubbing her arm where his fingers had been, the skin still stung.

After all this time, just when she was starting to not think about Lucas...

While she hated him, she still found herself lusting after him. At night in her dreams it was Lucas who was touching her, kissing her. Damn him! He was becoming a thorn in her backside!

The picture of Lucas kissing her showed up in every gossip magazine but *Tainted*. Her new studio called her in for a meeting the next afternoon. It was like a bad rerun to last time she got caught kissing Lucas.

"The benefactor for the studio is strict about what press a dancer is covered in. The gossip columns are not one of them, Miss Kelly," her head teacher was saying.

"I understand, Mr. Lava, but I didn't ask for the kiss," Alexa explained.

"It doesn't matter, Miss Kelly. The story is out now. You will do an extra program for the studio, and this is all the action we will take."

"What is this is extra program about?" Alexa asked.

"You will get a detailed outline of the dance for this program later. For now we ask you to please avoid getting your name tangled in with gossip."

Alexa's week quickly took a turn for the worse. By Thursday she was ready to have a mental breakdown! The picture kept showing up, reminding her how Lucas had managed to screw with her once again.

The icing on the cake came on Friday when she got the outline for the new ballet performance she would have to do. Her jaw dropped as she read the storyline.

A girl paints herself up as a lady of the night to spy on a wealthy man. When she gets what she wants, she turns on him and thinks she can get away with it. Yet the man she ruined ends up being far more powerful than she could have ever imagined and she becomes trapped in his twisted plot of revenge, losing everything she holds dear.

Alexa didn't fancy herself a paranoid kind of person, but with the outline of the new performance so spot on with what had happened with Lucas, she had to wonder what kind of game the studio was playing. Where they teaching her a lesson? It had to be the reason for the story. Clearly they were sending her a message.

It had to be. The other option for it was not a good one. If she let her mind wander to the only other reason she would be dancing a ballet written to the plot of one of her biggest mistakes, it would lead to her being extremely paranoid.

Lucas Kane had somehow blackmailed his way into her world and was messing with her in the one place she should be safe from him. Alexa closed her eyes but all she could see was the words: *Far more powerful then she could have ever imagined… trapped in his twisted plot of revenge, losing everything she holds dear.*

And for once, Alexa and her inner voice were in agreement. *We're screwed!*